Nuala O'Connor (AKA Nuala Ní Chon... and lives in East Galway. A novelist, short st... the author of three novels, including *Miss Em...* Sandstone (UK)), about the poet Emily Dickinson and her Irish maid, five short story collections, and four collections of poetry. *Miss Emily* was shortlisted for the Novel of the Year award at the 2015 Irish Book Awards, and longlisted for the 2017 International DUBLIN Literary Award. Nuala's fourth novel, *Becoming Belle*, is published in 2018.

www.nualaoconnor.com

Praise for *Miss Emily*

'There can be no better pairing than the great American poet Emily Dickinson recreated through the magical imagination of Irish writer Nuala O'Connor ... *Miss Emily* is mesmerizing from its first pages, a feat made possible only by the pen of a writer of immense talent who connects with Dickinson. She writes from the poet's perspective with utter confidence, without cliché and with the same love of words. A gift indeed.' – Linda Diebel, *Toronto Star*

'Nuala O'Connor's lovely novel pulls us in from its first limpid lines and then detonates with an explosion of power – much like Emily Dickinson's poems. The novel captivates with its high emotions and rich images. Hope, Ada comments, 'may be small and bald at first, but then it gathers feathers to itself and flies on robust wings.' So, too, does O'Connor's quietly soaring novel.' – Heller McAlpin, *Washington Post*

'O'Connor brings one of America's most beloved poets to life. [She] is a gifted writer; not only does she bring a believable sense of poetry (clay is "deathly cool around my fingers") and self-assurance to Emily, she is also capable of conveying complex feeling succinctly, a talent shared by her historical heroine. This novel has the possibility of being a book club juggernaut.' – Starred review in *Publishers Weekly*

'… beautifully and convincingly evokes the startling, luminous world captured in Dickinson's poems …' – John G. Matthews, Washington State Univ. Libs., Pullman in *Library Journal*'s July 2015 issue

'Irish writer Nuala O'Connor breathes new life into reclusive poet Emily Dickinson in her mesmerizing U.S. debut. Like one of Dickinson's poems, the deceptively simple narrative packs a powerful punch.' – Margaret Flanagan, Booklist

'Dickinson in Nuala O'Connor's revelatory American debut novel Miss Emily. O'Connor's narrative is no small feat, bringing together the life of Dickinson the poet and her fictional Irish maid Ada Concannon. What follows is a moving and often engrossing tale of the bonds of friendship, the power of language, and the intricacies of the human heart.' – Irish America Review

'All aspects of the book – characterization, prose, setting and storyline – are in top form, setting this author apart from many who take on a rehash of a well-known and documented historical figure. Lyrical and beautifully written, this story should not be missed by fans of Emily Dickinson, or anyone simply looking for a great historical read.' – Historical Novels Review

'… Nuala O'Connor's excellent *Miss Emily* which gave us a wilful and tormented Emily Dickinson.' – Alex Preston, *The Guardian*

'This accomplished novel is deftly structured. In its economy of scale it may deliberately emulate a Dickinson poem … a lyrical and thoroughly readable novel with a compelling storyline.' – Éilís Ní Dhuibhne, *The Irish Times*

'This charming novel, full of baking aromas and household hints … as well as darker almost deathly episodes, returns towards the end to a lovely, untamed buoyancy …' – Penny Perrick, *Sunday Times*

'… O'Connor is overdue a larger audience for her carefully crafted fiction that gut-punches the reader with its honesty and emotion … the author goes deep into her characters to offer a meditation on the human condition.' – Sarah Gilmartin, *Sunday Business Post*

'*Miss Emily* gains considerable pace towards its finale, and is a satisfying and enjoyable read from one of Ireland's more unsung talents, who deserves to make the step to a much wider readership.' – Desmond Traynor, *Sunday Independent*

'A superb novel, I was captivated from the first page. With gorgeous, compelling period detail and graceful prose, Nuala O'Connor reimagines a friendship between one of our greatest poets and her Irish maid ... O'Connor celebrates her women with great delicacy and exuberance.' – Kathleen Grissom, bestselling author of *The Kitchen House*

'I read this wonderful novel in a gulp. Nuala O'Connor is a gifted storyteller with a poet's eye for detail ... I can't wait to read what O'Connor writes next.' – Natasha Solomons, *New York Times* bestselling author of *The House at Tyneford*

'Beautifully written and utterly compelling, this vivid portrait of Emily Dickinson examines her humanity, complexity and profound relationship with words ... *Miss Emily* deftly braids together the stories of two intriguing women in this highly accomplished novel.' – Cathy Marie Buchanan, *New York Times* bestselling author of *The Painted Girls*

'Nuala O'Connor's *Miss Emily* is evocative, thought-provoking, and beautifully rendered ... Readers will delight in this richly imagined glimpse into the worlds – both inner and outer – of the immortal Emily Dickinson. I wanted to race through the novel, and yet, the language was so engrossing that I forced myself to slow down, just enough to savor each sentence.' – Allison Pataki, *New York Times* bestselling author of *The Traitor's Wife* and *The Accidental Empress*

'*Miss Emily* is a triumph of a novel, creating an utterly human and believable Emily Dickinson through the eyes of an enchanting and complex fictional Irish woman ... Nuala O'Connor has long been one of my favorite contemporary Irish writers.' – Pulitzer Prize-winning author Robert Olen Butler

'A jewel of a novel ... With its luminous prose and sympathetic, realistically drawn characters, you will feel yourself irresistibly drawn into Emily's and Ada's private worlds with every turn of the page.' – Syrie

James, bestselling author of *Jane Austen's First Love* and *The Lost Memoirs of Jane Austen*

'I lost myself in the beautiful detail of 1860s Amherst, a cast of characters that leapt off the page with life, and the constant reminder that words, properly wielded, can transcend time, transmit love, and, above all, inspire hope.' – Charlie Lovett, *New York Times* bestselling author of *The Bookman's Tale*

'In the same way as Emily Dickinson's poems were once the best kept secret in Massachusetts, Nuala O'Connor's luminous prose has long been one of Ireland's most treasured literary secrets ... Through a fusion of historical ventriloquism and imaginative dexterity, O'Connor vividly conjures up ... two equally unforgettable characters who pulsate with life ...' – Dermot Bolger

Praise for *The Closet of Savage Mementos*

'... the poet's aesthetic and linguistic sensitivity is evident throughout ... She doesn't flinch when tackling the dark truths of human behaviour, the savage mementos at the heart of family relationships and growing up. Earlier work has drawn comparisons to Edna O'Brien. With her ability to get inside a story, and a writing style that is both lyrical and exact, it is easy to see why.' – *The Irish Times*

'This isn't a story of sparkle and bling; there are no cosy fire-side chats, fun shopping sprees or drunken parties. It is raw, beautiful and compelling, a 'must read'.' – *The Sunday Independent*

'... her finest novel yet.' – *The Sunday Times*

'Compelling and deeply accomplished, *The Closet of Savage Mementos* is the product of a powerful literary talent.' – *The Evening Echo*

'It is difficult to write sex well, but Ní Chonchúir manages to strike a delicate balance between passion and poetry.' – *The Sunday Business Post*

'... this engaging book ... this most readable novel.' *Irish Independent*

Praise for *Mother America*

'I'm going through this [book] slowly, reluctant to leave its atmosphere of blended light and shadow.' – Helen Oyeyemi, *The Guardian*

'... Ní Chonchúir, like Frida Kahlo, documents female lives in ripe, uncompromising detail. I was also reminded of Edna O'Brien to whose groundbreaking work most Irish women writers owe a debt. Ní Chonchúir's precisely made but deliciously sensual stories mark her as a carrier of the flame.' – *The Irish Times*

'... the prose is measured and graceful, rich with delectable turns of phrase and vivid descriptions that seem to paralyse time ... Over the past decade, Miss Ní Chonchúir has proven herself a prolific and diverse talent.' – *The Irish Examiner*

'... Ní Chonchúir ... immediately arrests the reader's attention with jolting declarations, oddities and intriguingly out-of-place ideas ... A short, satisfying read, *Mother America* offers shards of humour and solace in a collection primarily concerned with the complexities of love ... in the difficult task of writing about sex, the author shows particular flair.' – *The Sunday Times*

'*Mother America* is a collection that deserves attention and praise not only for its author's mastery of her craft, but also for its poignant language and complexity of human bonding. Reliability lies in the dichotomy between darkness and light, or revelation and obscurity that Woolf so well identified in short story language – and which is a major source of strength for Nuala Ní Chonchúir.' – *The Brazilian Journal of Irish Studies*

'Ní Chonchúir's bravery in forcing her reader to plunge directly into dark waters of the unexpected, the taboo and the downright ugly aspects of motherhood and family, combined with the powerful intimacy of her prose, make hers a literary voice which should and will be heard.' – *The Short Review*

Praise for *YOU* (novel)

'... *You* deserves to find a place in our pantheon of much-admired, beautifully crafted variations on a theme.' – *The Irish Times*

'... timeless, placeless and universal ... a must read.' – *The Irish Independent*

'... a vivid and immediate sensory experience ... Ní Chonchúir's ear – as you might expect of a poet – is alive to the language of her characters ... it is about the ordinary, and the secret life that runs beneath it.' *The Sunday Business Post*

'The novel flows beautifully and is understated in tone ... This gem is sure to win her further acclaim. Nuala Ní Chonchúir is a writer to watch.' – *The Irish Examiner*

'*You* supplies a pitch-perfect voice to the estranged youngster within each of us, the result being a quietly disarming experience for the reader...It is another success from a writer who seems composed of something that literary awards like to be around ... It's all done organically, the hand of the author combining with the reader's own sense of childhood nostalgia to create literary alchemy.' – *Sunday Independent*

'Ní Chonchúir is excellent on the shifting allegiances between children ... this would not have been taken for a début.' – *Sunday Tribune*

Joyride to Jupiter

Joyride to Jupiter

stories

Nuala O'Connor

NEW ISLAND

JOYRIDE TO JUPITER
First published in 2017 by
New Island Books
16 Priory Hall Office Park
Stillorgan
County Dublin
Republic of Ireland

www.newisland.ie

Print ISBN: 978-1-84840-615-5
Epub ISBN: 978-1-84840-616-2
Mobi ISBN: 978-1-84840-617-9

British Library Cataloguing Data.

A CIP catalogue record for this book is available from the British Library.

Typeset by JVR Creative India
Cover design by Mariel Deegan

New Island received financial assistance from The Arts Council (*An Chomhairle Ealaíon*), 70 Merrion Square, Dublin 2, Ireland.

New Island Books is a member of Publishing Ireland.

MIX
Paper from
responsible sources
FSC® C013056
www.fsc.org

Printed and bound in Great Britain by
TJ International Ltd, Padstow, Cornwall

For The Peers, who always help

'Jupiter from on high smiles at the perjuries of lovers.'

Ovid

Contents

Joyride to Jupiter

The year was set up wrong from the start – wavering sun on New Year's Day and snow on the seventeenth of March that stopped every parade from Malin to Mizen. I didn't know the whole thing would fall asunder, but I knew something was going to go wrong, as sure as I knew west was west.

I first took notice at Eastertime when Teresa disrupted the plans for our traditional dinner. We were at the kitchen table, making our shopping list.

'We won't have any of that yoke,' she said, waving her pen. 'What do you call it? Legs, you know. Woolly. It jumps.' She leapt in her seat and laughed; I was startled – it was a move so unlike her. 'Woolly little fellas,' she said, and wiggled her fingers.

'Are you talking about lambs?'

'Lamb!' She seized the word like a biblical wolf. 'Lamb. Yes. None of that.'

So it started that way. Teresa began to change her mind about things that were sacred to her: there were no more fire-and-wine Friday nights. No more wedge heels or skirt suits. And she wanted sweet food to eat above all else: custard, Petits Filous, Jelly Tots.

One Saturday morning I asked if she was going to the hair salon; she had missed two Saturdays by then.

1

'Is it salon or saloon?' she said. 'I've always wondered about that. I'm beginning to think it's saloon.' She made a gun of her fingers. 'Bang bang!' She cackled and I sat in my armchair and looked at her, wondering what was happening to us.

At first I thought Teresa must have found another man and she was changing for his pleasure, but she was never missing, never anywhere but at work or at home. Then she retired from work abruptly and gusted about the house putting things in odd places – loo roll in the drinks cabinet, frozen peas under the stairs. And she hummed high, pointless tunes all the time. She talked less, too, as if words didn't hold weight anymore.

The push-me-pull-you of married life, all the compromises and stand-offs, were waning. She became separate and distant but I was not going to give up on Teresa, not at all. So I got a girl to come in to help me – Marguerite – and she's gentle with Teresa, a gift.

'How's the form, Mr Halpin?' Marguerite says, bustling in the door in the mornings, all wide-hipped and capable.

'You make me feel old with your "Mr Halpin",' I tell her.

'The thing is, Mr Halpin, you *are* old.'

That's the way Marguerite is, straight as a runway. But she cherishes Teresa, keeps her voice low and coaxing with her, and Teresa smiles, accepts Marguerite's firm, friendly assistance in a way that is contrary to the woman I married. My Teresa never wants help; she's a one woman show.

Before her mind sagged, Teresa was bad at being sick – a play actor. She took pleasure in her performance as Disgruntled Patient. She luxuriated over tablet taking – lined them up like gems to be admired. Each headache foretold a brain haemorrhage, every leg creak was bone cancer. She endured but enjoyed hospital visits, complaining non-stop. Now she is truly sick and she neither knows nor cares. My poor, wandering girl.

This morning I found Teresa standing by the chest of drawers in a vest and nothing else. She had taken off the pants and blouse I'd dressed her in an hour before.

'What are you doing, sweetheart?' I said.

'I can't find my tracksuit.'

'You don't have a tracksuit, Teresa.'

She wrinkled her nose and made slits of her eyes. This we called her angry koala face and, when I used to say, 'Oh, the angry koala is here', it melted things, and the koala went back up its tree. But Teresa continued to frown, thinking – if she thinks much at all – that I was thwarting her.

'Tracksuit,' she said.

'I'll tell you what, why don't I go to Penneys and get you a tracksuit? When Marguerite gets here.'

'Marguerite? Who's that?'

And then she laughed because laughter falls from her now as it never did; it falls and pools around us, the one good thing. I knelt and stepped her feet into her knickers and pulled them up. I put her arms into the sleeves of her blouse and fiddled with the tiny buttons. She was childlike in her pliancy. I kissed her forehead.

'You're my dolly,' I said.

She put her arms around my neck and we held each other for a long time.

I started my jaunts, on the little train that snakes up and down the shopping centre, shortly after I found Marguerite. She said I should get out of the house. 'Out from under my feet' was what she actually said. Today Marguerite isn't here so I have to bring Teresa with me to the shops. The train driver sees us; he waves and stops the engine.

'All aboard,' he says, tipping his head towards the carriages. He asks where we're headed and I tell him. 'Sit tight and I'll spin you down.'

Teresa sits with her hands folded in her lap, staring regally at the shoppers sloping through the centre. It is the same expression that shy children wear when they sit on the little train – they want to be there, enjoying the trip, but it embarrasses them too because people turn to look, they smile and wave. These are the kids I love the most. They are rooted in themselves and they shoulder the world warily, like I did as a child.

We sit in our tiny compartment and I sing a verse to Teresa, from a song we knew as youngsters:

The Dingle train is whistling now
'Tis time to make the tay.
That's what they said in Tralee town
When evening came the way.

She looks at me like she has never heard this before, so I sing it again, trying to plunge the tune into her mind, willing her to sing along.

The Dingle train is whistling now
'Tis time to make the tay ...

In Penneys Teresa stands in front of the make-up rack, picking up lipsticks and pots of eyeshadow and blusher; she is contained, at a distance from everything. She never did have that Irish capacity to linger, after dinner or at pub closing time – when she was done with a place she was done, and we were always the first to leave a gathering. But, in her new state, she idles over everything, examining and waiting, with stores of patience that weren't hers before. I leave her and do my bit of shopping with one eye clamped on her. She stands, studying the make-up containers with care. I come back and, when Teresa sees me, she hands over the little pots one at a time. I read out their names to her, before pressing them back into their slots.

'Sparkling Miracle. Glamour Queen. Mystic Purple. Yes Eye Can! Nude Candy. Fairytale. Disco Diva. Joyride to Jupiter.' Joyride to Jupiter makes her laugh like a girl – a sweet gurgle from her throat – and I hold it up and ask, 'Would you like this?'

'Can I have it?' She takes the small tub of eyeshadow and clutches it as if it's a jewel from Derrynaflan. 'Joyride to Jupiter,' Teresa says, looking at it in wonder.

I am the worm in the dementia apple; I will tunnel through it, I will not let it get the better of us. Everything is different, and will be different, but there are things I can hang on to.

I take Teresa to our bedroom. The room smells of talc and dirty socks; it has always smelt like this. I undress her with care, tumble out of my own clothes, and we tuckle under the duvet. Her skin is buttermilk soft and I hold her close and caress the neat hollow in her back.

'Chancing your arm, as usual,' she says.

'You love it,' I say.

She presses her breasts to my chest and heat rushes through the length of me. I have long treasured the honesty of our lovemaking; we could always look each other in the eye in the middle of it all and grin, heated up though we were. That hasn't changed, though she gazes at me with bewilderment sometimes now. But she looks happily bewildered, because I know what to do to make her feel good and she responds as she always did, with grunts of pleasure and fierce kisses.

Afterwards we eat. This has been our ritual for fifty years. Today I have a bowl of cherries beside the bed and I de-pip them one at a time with my lips and, like a bird, I drop the soft flesh into Teresa's mouth. She sucks and chews the scarlet pulp and smiles up at me. It pleases me somehow that she is childlike; she is the girl I courted and won. Gone is the snappy, impatient Teresa she grew into. Back is good-natured, sunny Teresa.

The children on the train in the shopping centre are often plump. I love that slight pudginess that most kids have, their hands 'swollen with candy' as the song goes. Sometimes, when they are struggling to board, I lift them into their seats and their cushiony flesh amazes me. How so soft, so yielding? If my hands stay a little too long on their fat waists they shrug me off, impatient to take their seats. A mother gives me a sharp look from time to time.

But it's worth it for the sweet feeling imprinted on my hands.

I travel up and down on the train for hours at a time. The driver doesn't mind; he only ever charges me one fare. Once, instead of going to the shopping centre, I went to Heuston Station and took a real train as far as Portarlington. I squinted through the window – a hump in a field was either a very small cow or a very large rabbit; either way I didn't care, these views didn't interest me. The muffled Tannoy announcements were irritating too; it took me ages to figure out what the announcer was saying. I heard 'sex and savages' for 'snacks and beverages'. I drank mushroomy, caramel-tinged tea from a paper cup and paid €2.10 for the experience. No, all in all I prefer my little shopping centre train to the real thing. There are better things to see from it, like the balloon man and the sweetie cart and all the children with their families who trundle about together, lost in a miasma of fast-food and squandered money.

Our daughter comes to visit; she doesn't come much – some long-nursed wariness of me keeps her away. She turns up less and less since Teresa began to flounder; since she began to forget things and wander and dress strangely.

'Seven walnuts a day, that's what she needs,' our daughter says to me. 'Seven walnuts a day, Mam, OK?' she half-shouts at her mother.

'Oh, yes,' Teresa says, as if this makes sense to her. She blinks at our daughter, trying to place her.

'Walnuts?' I ask.

'For her memory,' she says. 'They have polyphenolites or something. Anyway, I read something and it said they'd

7

help.' She plucks at the hood of Teresa's tracksuit top with her fingers. 'What in God's name is she wearing? It's beat onto her; she'd be mortified if she could see herself.'

'Your mother asked me for it. She wanted it. And she can look in the mirror any time she wants to see herself.'

Our daughter pokes through the things on the top of the chest of drawers, to distract herself from Teresa, who is perched on the bed in her pink velour tracksuit, looking ridiculous and wrong but content.

'What is this shite? Eyeshadow?' our daughter says, holding up the pot of Joyride to Jupiter. 'This stuff is total crap. It's for teenagers.'

Teresa barrels across the room and slaps our daughter's cheek, *phwack*. She grabs the eyeshadow and pockets it. The three of us stand, suspended.

'Jesus, Mam.' Our daughter holds her cheek and moves towards Teresa but I wedge myself between them.

'She was a good mother to you,' I say. 'A good mother. She needs your respect.'

'What she *needs* is to be in a home. A hospital. Somewhere.' Our daughter grabs her handbag and heads across the room. She turns. 'But you, you selfish old prick, you have to have it your own way, as usual. She needs help.' She slams the door.

'She has help,' I say, pulling Teresa close to me. 'You're OK, aren't you? My girl, my love.'

The pub is not the kind of pub I like; it's manufactured, unorganic. Even the barmen look plastic. I sit, feeling stiff, on a green leather banquette, under a television screen the size of a car. But the pub is here for the convenience of the shopping centre and, today – my first time here – it is certainly convenient. I sup a lager then gulp another. I crunch through a bag of bitter nuts and read a discarded *Herald*. More lager and then a Jameson, to pile sour upon sour.

Very little makes me happy anymore and, conversely, it takes very little to make Teresa madly happy. It's all topsy-turvy. Teresa was a terror, really, before; the girls she worked with were afraid of her and probably didn't like her much. Not one of them has come to see her, or rung her, since she left the job. Not one.

I down the last of the whiskey. By the time I take my place on the little train, my ears are buzzing and my stomach doesn't feel the best. A slender girl with huge grey eyes takes the seat beside me.

'Hello,' I say.

'Hi.'

'And what's your name, little lady?'

'Mary-Kate.'

'You're not serious?' I place my hand on her leg. 'I had a dog called Mary-Kate once. A big fucking ugly wolfhound. A horrible bitch, she was.'

The girl's face contorts and I put my arm around her. 'Not to worry,' I say. 'She's dead now. Dead as door-knobs, Mary-Kate.'

'Mam,' the girl says, a plaintive squeak as she looks over her shoulder for her mother.

The train lurches forward and my belly gets left behind until it lands in my throat and I throw-up, all over myself and the train and small, grey-eyed Mary-Kate.

'There's a crow I want to pick with you, Mr Halpin,' Marguerite says, meeting me in the hallway.

'Oh, yes?' I have a wogeous headache; the hangover is already pounding through my body and it is barely two o'clock. I can still feel the pinch of the security guard's fingers braceleting my arm.

The train driver came to my defence.

'Leave him go,' he said, putting his hand on the security guard's chest. 'Are you all right?' he asked me.

I swayed and retched, muttered, 'Sorry, sorry,' over and over. I tried to wipe the sick from my jacket.

'You're barred,' the security man said. 'Do you hear me? Don't let me catch you near the place again.' He walked me to the exit.

I spotted a single coral rose blooming from a patch of dirt at the shopping centre's door. I plucked it.

'You can't take that,' the security man said.

'Watch me,' I said. He lunged for the rose and I ran. When I got near the bus stop I slowed to a trot. I walked home, carrying the flower for Teresa in front of me like a chalice.

'Mr Halpin? Are you all right?' Marguerite says, taking my arm.

'I'm grand, grand.'

She puts her hands on her hips. 'You never told me Teresa was going into Emerald Sunsets.'

'She isn't.'

'Well, that's not what your daughter says. She was here earlier looking for Teresa's pension book. She says Teresa has a place in the home from next month.'

I sit on the bottom of the stairs and weep. I know already that I will acquiesce.

The driveway up to Emerald Sunsets is a blood valley of fuchsia. Teresa and I sit in the back; our daughter drives, glances at me in the rear-view.

'It's just to orientate her. Give her a feel for the place,' she says.

I grunt.

The three of us walk around the home behind the owner. I gag on the faecal smell and hang back when we intrude on the rooms of sleeping residents. There is a horrible calm to the place.

'We'll make sure Mrs Halpin gets the best of rooms, the best of care,' the owner says, a line she spools out for every family no doubt.

'See, it's lovely,' our daughter says, once we're back in her car. 'She'll settle in no time.'

I take Teresa's hand in mine and say nothing.

Teresa sits on the bed; I pull her nightdress over her head. She giggles and nods.

'You have a lovely smile,' she says. I want to cry because that was one of the first things she ever said to me when we met at a dance in the Banba Hall.

I make love to her slowly and carefully, enjoying every press of her body. I push my hands into her hair and feel her breath on my neck; it's like nothing has changed. She is my girl, my small thing, my tender, yielding doll. There has always been a softness about Teresa and me. Some couples look like they'd break each other

11

in bed but not us; we always left our spiky selves at the bedroom door.

Afterwards I hand her a paradise square and she nibbles at it, pulls out the sultanas with her fingers, licks the jam and savours the cake's almond tang. When she has finished her cup of tea I pat her lips with a napkin and she lies back.

'There now, Teresa,' I say and am glad of the ease of her, the quiet, contented peace.

Soon she drifts and settles, her little silver head quiet beside me. I lift my pillow. Teresa pushes and fights; I stop, think of letting go, but I grip the sides of the pillow tighter and carry on. I hold it down, push my own face into the top of it and sob. Then, jerk one. Jerk two. And she's gone. I pull the pillow off her face and take her in my arms until I fall asleep myself.

The detritus of my mind gets locked down in dreams – Emerald Sunsets, paradise squares, our daughter's nervous glancing in the rear-view, waltzes in the Banba Hall, a single coral rose, the spongy hump of the pillow. And though Teresa is safe in my arms, even in my dream-drenched sleep, I know she is gone from me.

Consolata

I drive up the avenue and the trees dip low over the car, conjuring my childhood. I'm glad to see them so full and free. I glimpse the serried clutter of black crosses in the field beyond the hedge – the simple graves belonging to the convent next door. The nuns' plot was my playground as a girl but I would dash, wary, back to our orchard if I glimpsed a grey habit. Young Sister Consolata, though, often managed to waylay me; she was tiny and fresh, not at all like the other nuns. She liked to plait my hair and tell me things and, sometimes, I let her.

Daddy always said our apples were blessed because the order lived beside us. He liked to gift crates of Egremont Russets, the sweetest of all his fruit, to the sisters; we always called Egremonts 'nun apples' at home. The orchard shut down after he died and, though my mother can't quite believe she has no money anymore, she doesn't care much either. Her family set up my parents with the house and its land before they married and Daddy made a good go of the business. But, when he was gone, it was all too much for Mam and the place deteriorated until she was forced to close.

I park the car by the front of the house and turn to Matthew. 'This is it,' I say.

He leans across me to look through the windscreen. 'It's fucking huge.'

I look at the lofty Queen Anne-ish façade rising up over three floors. 'It is, I suppose.'

We go around the back, the front door being for high days only, which Good Friday, in our family, is not. Mam is slumped in an ancient deck chair in the yard and she looks undone. She sits, hand a-dangle above a mug of homemade cider, as if some mighty bird is about to swoop down and whisk it up into the clouds. She has probably sat here all day.

Squinting up at me with one languid eye, the other closed, she says, 'I hope, Helen, you're not expecting tea. There's nothing reasonable to eat in the house.'

'Did Patsy not get your messages?' I ask.

She flaps her hand. 'Sure, she's useless.'

'Mam,' I say, 'this is Matthew.' He steps forward to be inspected, and my mother offers only a salute; the uncharacteristic spring heat seems to do away with her need for words. 'And this is Verona, my mother.'

'It's lovely to meet you, Verona.' Mam sips her cider and nods, her disinterest interesting to me because I've been harassed in the past about boyfriends, my mother snuffling after me like a resolute badger, wanting to meet them. 'We brought oysters,' Matthew says, after a silence that clings.

'Of course you did,' Mam says. 'Have a sup of cider, Matthew, I made it myself. Helen, get glasses.'

I go through the boot room to the kitchen and, not finding any glassware in the press, I pluck two cups from the draining board; they are, of course, hennaed with tannin but I hope Matthew won't mind. The kitchen has its familiar rotten-onion, stale-biscuit smell and I wonder about bringing Matthew into the house, about what he'll make of its chaos of bric-a-brac and sail-like cobwebs, its peculiar air. I come out the back door to the yard and stand to watch the sun drift west. I go to the old sink, heave my mother's demi-john of cider out of its water bath, and pour.

'I made a simnel cake,' my mother says.

'Did you?' I say, surprised by this unusual marking of the occasion.

'And I fired Patsy.'

'Ah, Mam, not again. How will you manage?'

'I'm alive, amn't I?' She leans over and knocks her mug against Matthew's. '*Sláinte agus táinte*, young Matthew. I hope you're ready for this one.' She nods at me.

'I am,' Matthew says. 'Ready etcetera.'

He grins and I'm grateful for his contained ease. I've been uptight about this visit, worried that by meeting Mam, and being in the house, he'll see into me in a way I won't welcome. Matthew is perched on the back step and I sit beside him. My mother whistles a line of 'Eleanor Rigby' and looks off into the sunset like a pilgrim contemplating a promised land. She's a dyed-in-the-wool loner and I know me and Matthew being here may be hard on her – the having to converse, the need for civility. My mother is unused to the company of outsiders and doesn't welcome it.

'Yep, just me and the house now,' she says, as if catching my thoughts.

'So, Patsy's gone again. What did she try to appropriate this time?' I ask.

'The portrait of your father. Not the ugly one.'

I tut. 'You should've let her have it.'

'I did let her have it. But I got rid of her, too.'

'She'll be back, I suppose.'

Mam shrugs and grins. She has taken to her role as singleton, as unsentimental widow, with an inert joy; she seems determined to live her life now in unfettered nonchalance. Patsy, who had always acted as a lopsided buffer between Mam and Daddy, was clearly extraneous. Patsy's loyalty to my father was fierce, but it was my mother she was left with. My parents' marriage didn't age well, there was a certain disgust for each other in all interactions towards the end. Daddy was one of those men who embraced the arrogance of his generation, he was never afraid to use a domineering charisma in order to get his way. He cajoled Patsy like a snake-charmer and she sucked it up. Despite his overbearance, despite his lumpen shape, women always liked Daddy. He begrudged the young – me – their very youth, as he got older. Women of his own generation, like Patsy, were his preferred companions because they knew how to acquiesce. My mother, being contrary, never kow-towed to him. I look at her now and it's clear to me that she has thrown off Daddy like a shackle, that without him – and without Patsy too – she has found a way to be somewhat content. Well, she is a woman who thrives alone so perhaps she is better off.

The cider is flat, but cool and welcome slipping down my throat. The heat that radiates from Matthew's body, beside me on the step, brings back our morning in my bed: the slick, fierce weight of him on top of me, the sweet length of him inside me, his soft grunts and smiles.

I quiver and goose flesh stipples my arms, despite the heat that drapes the yard.

My father would have baulked at our inertia, even today; though he was basted in religion, he didn't approve of holy days. His annoyance at perceived laziness could be spectacular at times and I spent my young life on edge, ready to ward off his fury if he found me idle when the orchard was busy. Every season had its chores and Daddy meant to see we all took part in them, the better to produce the finest fruit in County Dublin.

My mother sips her cider and belches quietly between each draught. 'The nun apples are even sweeter since your father died,' she says.

'You might be right,' I answer; she has overheard my thoughts again it seems.

'Amn't I always right?' she murmurs.

The sun's heat sends my mind adrift. I gaze across the yard and wonder if the ferocity of new love can ever last. My parents surely once loved as I love now? If Matthew and I stay together, will I always want to coil up on his chest after sex? In five years, say, will I still relish the scatter of hair in the small of his back that I stroke like a pet while he sleeps? And will he hold me all night, pursuing me across the sheets when I try to ease away? I take Matthew's hand in mine and kiss each knuckle in turn; he smiles and pucks me gently with his side.

'Will we have supper?' I ask.

'Supper, no less,' Matthew says, and he and my mother laugh conspiratorially, as if at some marvellous joke.

'Her father's word,' Mam says, '"supper". That man always had a great idea of himself.'

'You miss him,' I say, and she snorts a denial. But she does miss Daddy, in her own way, despite everything. He's too often mentioned, too frequently summoned like a wisp of necessary air. She may be having a harder time letting go of him than she fancies.

I get up and go through the house to the car, pull the ice-box from the boot and haul it to the kitchen. I scrub the oysters in the sink and arrange them on a platter. They look elemental against the blue china, their fluted shells like pastry made of shale. My mouth drips in anticipation of the plump, briny meat. I put tea-lights in saucers along the table, cut lemons into wedges, and butter some brown bread.

'Mam! Matthew!' I roar from my place at the counter. Then, mindful of Matthew, it occurs to me that not all families communicate by shouting and I go to the back door. 'The food is ready,' I say, polite as a maid.

Mam tries to rock herself out of the deck chair on a series of swings. She snarls at the effort and flops back. Matthew stands and my mother holds up her hands to him. With a familiarity that tickles me, he heaves her from the chair, grunting histrionically all the while, which makes her laugh.

'Madame Verona,' he says, and offers her his arm.

'Master Matthew,' she replies and takes it.

The kitchen is cool after the heat of the yard but the candle flames and lofty ceiling make a welcome theatre of the room. They take their places and I nip back outside for the demijohn and mugs. I stand to watch shadows gather over the graveyard and get an urge to go and walk the land around the plots. When

I was alone there as a child, the crosses made climbing frames for my dolls and oak leaves their beds. The giant yew in the corner was my den and I sat on a rock under the protection of its low branches, savouring the dank tranquillity it offered. I was a quiet child, silent often, and this was taken for belligerence, by my father, by Patsy. Mam left me be. I always loved the graveyard's peace as much as the rumble of disquiet I sensed from the women interred under the soil. I talked to them, wandering from cross to cross, to lie on the grass above where they lay, my face to the sky.

'What's your name and what did you die of?' I asked, and I fully fancied that I received answers.

Sister Bartholomew: 'Throat cancer.'

Sister Consolata: 'A broken heart.'

Sister Rosario Maria: 'Old age.'

Consolata was placid, an undemanding companion. She didn't talk much but she always admired my dolls and taught me things about nature. It was she who explained periods to me when she found me on my rock examining a brackish stain on the crotch of my knickers. I had thought I was dying. Consolata seemed old to me, unsexed by the veil, but she was younger than the other nuns in age, as much as in spirit. I wasn't frightened of her as I was of them.

I look out over the graveyard and wave my hand at the crosses, resolving to visit the dead sisters in the morning.

'Helen!' Mam's shout comes loud into the yard. 'Hell! My stomach is stuck to my back with the hunger. Get in here!'

I go back in, top up our cider cups, and sit. Matthew is relaxed, loading his plate as solemnly as a priest at his rituals; he looks at home and that pleases me. I shuck my first oyster and the pop when I turn the knife under the top-shell makes me shudder.

'Aaaah,' I say.

I cut the muscle and raise the shell, being careful not to spill the salty juice, and offer a hasty '*bon appétit*' to the others. Mam is readying her shucking tool and Matthew is crushing a lemon wedge. I turn the shell-lip to my mouth, slide the oyster in and massage it briefly with my teeth; I savour its brawny goodness in my throat and the dance of sea salt on my tongue.

'Mmmm,' I sigh, and set to work on another.

Matthew cuts his from the shell and lifts it to his mouth with a fork.

'Why so dainty?' I ask.

He shrugs and pops the meat onto his tongue, but he slurps the next one straight from the shell. When we've had six each, Matthew retrieves the rest of the oysters from the ice-box and we eat on. At the end of those, Mam emits a bountiful burp and lays her two hands across her stomach.

'That was an absolute feast,' she says. 'Wonderful. The last supper, a day late.' She chuckles. 'Ah, supper. Yes.'

I sip the cold, grassy cider, look at Matthew and Mam, and feel content. 'This is the calm way this house *should* be occupied,' I say.

'A quiet life is good for the bones. For the soul. Whatever that might be.' My mother raises her mug to Matthew and me.

Scarfs of mist hang over the graveyard and I wish I'd brought my phone to take pictures to show to Matthew, who is still asleep in my old bedroom. He would like the gothic look of the wraiths that will soon evaporate to leave a corpulent dew on the grass. The ecology of this place is sewn into me and I know how every season affects it: the stark of winter, this springy soak-and-grow, summer's glorious greens, autumnal mulch. I stand and survey the grounds, the vapoury mist, the crosses, the trees, and I'm lachrymosely grateful that the whole lot hasn't been lost under a housing estate.

I rub my head and groan. My tongue is tart-sweet and my eye sockets are taut, pulled down towards my stomach which rises, in turn, to meet the tension in my forehead, on a horrible comingle of cider and oysters. We had continued to drink into the early hours and I slept little. I woke Matthew when dawn fingered its way into my room, wanting to make love, but he could only keep his eyes open for a moment so I rolled away and got up, the bed groaning as if disinclined to let me go.

Now I make my way through the black crosses to the yew tree; it looks, at once, larger and smaller than it did when I made it my den. I slip under its umbrella of branches and see that my rock is still there. Until the autumn I turned twelve that rock acted as chair and table and thinking spot. And also as a prop for young Sister Consolata, the better for my father to fuck her.

I had been sent to look for Daddy in the orchard; there was something jammed in the apple scratter. Mam, worried it was a mouse that would cause contamination, had to stop pulping apples, and she sent me down among the trees to shout for my father, the only one with the knack to clear the scratter's innards. I wandered, kicking at boggy windfalls to see their brown bruises split. Every so often I would remember my mission and call out 'Daddy! Dad! Dada!' but I kept my voice low, preferring to eke out the moments that I was free from the endless pressing of apples. I looked in a lacklustre way for my father's outline among the trees but, not being able to see him, I slipped instead into the graveyard to confer with the dead. I wove through the crosses, touching their tips to greet the dead sisters below.

'Good day, Sister Bartholomew. Hello to you, Sister Rosario Maria.'

I headed to the yew tree to retrieve a book left there the day before. As I approached I heard a moist slap-slap and the same brutish groans that sometimes emanated from my parents' bedroom. I bent over to make myself small and didn't lift the branch canopy, but dipped under it to lie on the ground. I didn't realise at first that it was Consolata – her head was bare – all I saw was a person with straw-coloured hair, like my own, but cropped. She was draped backwards over my rock. My father was on top, pushing rhythmically and grunting. His balled fists held him up, and the fair head below him bounced and incanted, and Daddy leaned down on each thrust and kissed the face. Then the head bent further back and I saw who it was, saw the lips that said my hair was pretty as she combed it, the same mouth that told me the yew tree was toxic and to be careful under its cover.

'The yew's name, *taxus baccata*, means "toxic berry",' Consolata had said. 'And, Helen, you must never eat its berries, bright and soft though they are.'

I saw Sister Consolata's eyes open and they were glossy and large. My father continued his lunging movements and I whimpered to watch my friend beneath him. I was drawn to Consolata by her silence and yet here she was, invoking God, shout-whispering my father's name, whining like a feral cat. Never had I heard such odd noises from her before and I didn't like it one bit. My father's hands moved under her habit and he licked and snapped at her neck in great consuming lunges. The sister's breath came in delighted gasps until she focused on me, then she bucked her head upwards and twisted her body in my direction.

I jumped from the ground, shouted, '*Taxus baccata! Taxus baccata!*' and dashed back to the gap in the hedge to our orchard. I ran up through the trees towards the house and straight into the arms of Patsy who had been sent to look for my father and me.

'Whoa, Helen, whoa!' she roared and grabbed me to her. I was panting and outraged. How could Sister Consolata want to be better friends with my father than with me? Why would she let him put his tongue on her neck that way and kiss her? What possessed her to let him grind at her like an animal in heat? Patsy gripped my shoulders and held me away from her. 'What bee is in your bonnet, missy?'

'Daddy has Sister Consolata on my rock under the yew,' I said, 'and they're humping like two auld dogs!'

Patsy slapped my cheek hard then pulled me to her breast. She hugged me close and dropped her mouth to my ear. 'God will strike you dead if you ever say that again. Don't dare repeat it. To anyone. Do you hear me?'

I nodded and she pushed me away from her and set off down the orchard calling my father's name. I ran to the barn, bubbling with shame and rage. My mother was poking a broom handle into the scratter.

'Helen! Hell! Where did you get to?'

'Nowhere.'

'Did you find him?' I shook my head. 'Christ on a fucking bike, give me patience,' she said, and pulled the broom handle out and threw it to the floor.

Daddy and Patsy appeared in the barn doorway, both out of breath, both pantomiming calm.

'What is it, Verona?' Daddy said, walking forward to Mam. His glance didn't meet mine but the hum of his guilt flew into the barn with him and settled in the rafters above all our heads.

'That yoke,' Mam said, pointing at the scratter. 'I'm fit to take the hammer to it at this stage.'

'You'll do no such thing,' Daddy said, and went to the shelf for his toolbox.

Patsy looked at me and mouthed a 'No'. I eyed her and swallowed the words that scrambled in my gut, itching to be said.

Mam came over to me. 'What've you been up to, Hell? You look half mad.' She laughed and knocked muck off my knees with one palm.

'She was below in the orchard, missus,' Patsy said, 'idle as a cat.'

'As long as you weren't beyond the hedge, nun-bothering,' Mam said, pulling me to her side by my shoulder.

I looked from my father to Patsy. '*I* wasn't bothering anyone,' I said.

We are out in the yard again after a lunch of cheese and tomatoes and we cut Mam's simnel cake, its top a blaze of marzipan, dotted with sugar-shelled eggs.

'It's not like you to bake. To make a fuss about Easter.'

'With Patsy out from under my feet I can get up to all sorts,' she says.

She stands over Matthew and me and examines us.

'You look right together,' she says. 'Bless your youth. Bless your future.' She holds her mug and plate aloft like offerings. 'Eat this cake and drink this cider.'

So we do. And we sit, the three of us, and we talk about those who are buried and those who are yet to be born, and so much more besides. And while we talk I think about my father, about what his life meant and his death, and whether I will see him again in some dimension I don't yet understand, and if he'll explain himself to me. We sit on, us three, and we drink, talk and ponder it all until the April sun drops behind the orchard and is gone.

Yellow

At the entrance, a woman hands each of us a net. When I imagined this moment, I saw us being given a single net. We would move as one, four hands on the handle, catching our baby together.

'Twice the chance,' Rob hisses, snapping the net like a riding crop.

Yes, I think, *yes*. Double the opportunity. One hundred per cent better. Yes, yes!

We run side by side down the corridor, with all the other hopefuls, into the dome. I see babies high in the roof space, they helicopter and dive. The air smells of lotion and scalp. A Pink with seraphic thighs flies towards me and I shove past a man and try to net her. She dodges upwards and skims sideways. I jump high, knocking against the man again, but I miss.

'Get fucked!' the man screams at me and chases the Pink, arcing his net wildly but it meets empty air.

Up ahead I see Rob dip his net under a drifting Blue.

'Stop!' I shout, waving my arms. We agreed Pink and the rules are clear: one baby per couple. If Rob snags a Blue, it is over. 'What the hell are you at?' I scream. Rob steps back from the Blue and holds his palms out in surrender. 'Pink,' I snarl.

Then I see it, executing a cocky glissade above all the Pinks and Blues – a Yellow. Its face is turtlish but it looks strong. It seems unconcerned as it streels across the dome, surveying the waggle of a hundred nets and the anxiety of the would-be parents below. I catch the Yellow's eye and it holds my gaze.

'Come to me,' I whisper.

Keeping watch on its robust body, I see it gravitate towards me. The Yellow's eyes are clear and bright; it stares at me as if in recognition. I lift my net then let it fall to the floor. I open my arms and the Yellow descends, poised as a hawk. The baby's weight is so welcome and strange, and I am becalmed. The tiny parcel of unruly limbs settles and I hold it close.

The baby snuggles its head to my breast and Rob is suddenly at my side, placing his hand respectfully on the little one's beautiful head. We look at each other and smile. We look back at the baby. Our golden child. Our Yellow.

The Donor

The first time Xavier saw the child he was startled that the boy looked nothing like him. *My son*. He stood outside the school and gazed at him. No, there was not an ounce of him there. The boy looked like his mother: squat and sceptical. She – the mother – had a reality TV face; one of those faces that drips tears when her dough fails to prove, or her housemates vote her out.

'I was sure he would look like me,' Xavier complained to his sister Frances. 'Boys should look like their dads. The same way girls should never look like their dads. It's like a weird rule, you know?'

'But you're not his dad. Donors are not *dads*,' Frances said, shaking her plait to indicate annoyance, the same way she had since she was a girl.

The next time Xavier saw the child was after his first date with the boy's mother. *My son*. The mother was a noisy kisser. He didn't tell Frances that because, naturally, she would not approve of kissing, or any kind of contact, in fact. Frances was already angry with him for acting on the information she had provided from the clinic, where she was a receptionist.

'It is not cool to stalk a kid outside his school. *Très* not cool,' Frances had said, from her splayed-out position on their father's sofa, where she and Xavier were enduring their filial Sunday visit.

'Why did you give me the file then? What did you think I was going to do?'

'I dunno. I thought you just wanted to read it.'

'It was you who got me into the whole thing in the first place,' Xavier said.

Frances shrugged in agreement and popped another liquorice allsort between her teeth.

'Got you into what thing?' their father asked, and they both ignored him.

The boy's mother's name was Mary, but she liked to be called Singhi since she had started to follow a guru.

'I'm on a fast path to enlightenment,' she told Xavier, over a curry in Vindaloo Tindaloo, and he nodded. After that it was all 'My guru this' and 'My guru that'. 'My guru centres my chakras,' or some such shite. Xavier wasn't really listening to what Singhi said; he was eyeing her mouth thinking, I *know* about you. He wanted to say aloud, 'I *know* about you.' And, 'You own my son.' *My son.* Why, he wondered, does a woman like this go and buy sperm? But he already knew why. She had an ozone-sized hole in her psyche, or her bliss, or some bloody place. A hole she tried to plug by manifold means, one of which was motherhood. It's as if she won the boy in a raffle, Xavier thought.

The kissing didn't start until after the dinner, until after they had bussed back to Singhi's house. They stood at her front door and Xavier knew his son was inside and he wanted to get in. So he kissed Singhi and she kissed him back, resonantly, sloppily, suckily. Jesus Christ, no wonder she had to resort to vials and petri dishes and the syringed swimmers of a stranger. *My son.*

'Do you want to come inside?' Singhi asked.

'Sure,' said Xavier, trying to tone down his delight in case she took the wrong meaning.

The sitting room was all scarves pinned to the walls, woven throws on the sofa and jangly light fittings. And it had a smell – something ripe and unpleasant like old cheese. After the babysitter left, Xavier's son appeared at the bottom of the stairs, faux-sleepy, wearing *Mr Men* pyjama bottoms and nothing else. *My son.* The boy clearly roused himself to catch a look at his mother's visitor. Xavier gasped when he saw that the child's torso was identical to his own: pigeony and sallow. The boy's face, of course, was his mother's: big-lipped and – Xavier hated to think it – with a tilt that made him look unstable.

'Hello, little man,' Xavier said, wanting to moor the boy to the room. The child looked to his mother for clues.

'Ludo,' she said, 'this is Xavier.'

Ludo? She could not be serious. 'Ludo,' Xavier said. 'That's a curious name. Playful.'

The boy smiled, the same patronising grin that his mother wore. 'Ludo means "famous warrior",' the boy said, and slashed the air with an imaginary sword.

'Wow,' said Xavier, and he could already feel his interest in the child slipping, just as Frances had predicted.

'What the fuck are you doing this for?' Frances had said. 'You hate kids. I give you two months before you drop him.'

'Now,' Singhi intoned, clapping her hands. 'Up the wooden hill to Bedfordshire with you, Ludo. Xavier and I want to talk.' As she said this she winked and Xavier felt his bowels go slack.

The last time Xavier saw the child he studied him closely. Singhi had asked him to pick them up for a trip to the park. When she opened the door, a dog barrelled out of nowhere and flung itself at Xavier. He leapt to get out of its way.

'Jesus Christ!' Recovering himself he said, 'Is that your dog?' to the boy. Xavier stared at Ludo; really, when you looked at him properly, there wasn't a trace of Xavier or Frances or their parents there, not a whit. *My son ...*

Ludo hunkered down and began to talk absolute shite to the mutt. 'Beauty! Beauty! Thassa girl, thassa girl. Wuh wuh. There-she-is. Yes, there-she-is. Wuh wuh.' He let the dog lap his face and then tossed his head around like someone in love; Ludo even let it lick his mouth. Its name was Beauty, Xavier gathered, and he decided not to mention that he couldn't stand dogs. He wasn't sure if there was meant to be irony in the dog's name; it was a grey, puggy thing – mongrel from jaw to tail – and he truly had never seen an uglier mutt.

Ludo walked down the hallway, Beauty jumping crazily at his outstretched fingers, and Xavier shuffled behind. The house's meaty, hairy stink wrapped itself inside Xavier's nostrils like a disease. This wasn't quite the bonding dad-and-son encounter he had been hoping for.

'Meet Beauty,' Singhi said, smiling up at Xavier from the sofa, the dog between her legs, her fingernails scratching at its coat. Xavier whimpered a sort-of reply and looked at Singhi and Ludo. 'Beauty is not caused. It is. Did you know that, Xavier?'

'No, I can't say that I did.' He shoved his nose into his hand to escape the smell that crept like an aura around his head.

'Daddy gave Beauty to me,' Ludo said, and Xavier let his hand fall.

'Oh, really? Your daddy?'

'That's right,' Singhi said. 'She was a gift from Dieter.'

'Dieter?' Xavier squeaked.

'Dieter is Ludo's dad.' Seeing Xavier's expression, she pushed Beauty from her lap and stood in front of him. 'Oh, we're not together,' she said. 'Hey, you look a bit stressed out. Can I get you a chamomile tea?' Singhi cupped his elbows in her hands and pulled him towards her.

Xavier stepped back. 'You know, I'm not feeling great, I think I'd better go home and lie down, you know? Be in my own space.'

'What about our trip to the park? Ludo's been so excited about it.'

'Another time, yeah?'

Xavier stumbled back along the corridor and let himself out the front door. He stood with his back to Singhi and Ludo's house, his heart galloping in his chest. My son? he thought. *My* son? My *son*? *My son*?

The Boy from Petrópolis

I listen to the waltz of Lota's heart under my ear – *babumf, babumf, babumf.* The plump of the years when she might have borne children has fallen away. She is slender now, angular. I have not had a child either and so, between us, we own two wasted wombs, a pair of houses built but never occupied. I often wonder who is worse off – a motherless daughter, such as me; or the daughter who fails to become a mother, the one who ends the line. Also me. I am badly off on the double, perhaps. I lift myself off Lota and out of the bed. She will sleep on.

The new boy is outside the window when I enter the kitchen; the wheat of his hair is just visible above the sill. I open the back door.

'We gave you a key,' I say. 'You did not let yourself in.'

He stares at me and shakes his head. I repeat myself – my Portuguese is not sharp – and he shrugs. The boy is one of those sallow, green-eyed Brazilians, startling to look at. I didn't think anybody outside of fiction had such eyes but here he is, as green-eyed as a cat, or something more exotic – an ocelot, maybe. He has Germanic skin, smooth and healthy, the skin of someone who gets fresh air. His name is Tito da Silva, though he has half a dozen other names too, like everyone here.

I hand the mop to Tito and he sets off with it, slung rifle-wise over his shoulder. I have no idea where he is going but I don't call him back or quiz him. He will settle, I think; it won't take this one long to know what is what around here. I go through to my desk and sit. I poke at one typewriter key and watch its leg kick up and down like a can-can dancer. I look out the window; the milky blue of the sea is my constant distraction and this morning is no different. The water makes me long for the sway of a boat under my legs.

Something about Tito has set off a ripple in me and already I know I will not write a word. I gaze out the window, my chin cupped in my hand – like a *namoradeira* statue waiting for her lover – and watch the eddy and gush of the waves. The horizon sits high here, something I mull over often. Lota says it is to do with proximity to the equator and she is probably right. I imagine fish swishing down from that lofty horizon and crashing onto the shore on their bellies; shoals of fish, biblical and silver. I imagine myself among them.

'Madam, you did not give me a bucket.' Tito startles me and, when I turn to reprimand him, I see that he looks abashed, so I swallow my annoyance.

'It's "Miss"', I say, 'not "Madam". Please. Follow me.'

He trails behind me to the kitchen, head down. I hand him the bucket and he smiles. I sing: '*There's a hole in the bucket, dear Liza, dear Liza, there's a hole in the bucket, dear Liza, a hole.*' Tito steps away from me as if stung. 'It's just a silly old song,' I say. He stands, still and contained, looking at me as if indulging the half-mad. 'Go,' I say. 'Go mop.'

Back at my desk, I watch a lizard skitter down the garden path; it stops and tongues the air. I hope the cat will not saunter by and see it; he wouldn't hurt it but he likes to paw at lizards, toy with them. I wonder if it is the same lizard that found its way into our bed last week. It sat, a little regent, on Lota's pillow. I wanted to screech but knew that Lota wouldn't appreciate that; I squeaked and pointed.

'Come, friend,' she said, and carried the lizard, pillow and all, to the back door and set it free. The lizard ran, jerky and plastic, down the path.

I think this may be the same fellow; it certainly looks identical to our bedroom visitor. I watch the lizard's gait along the stones, its purposeful stop-and-start meander. Tito appears from nowhere, grabs the creature's tail and tosses it over the wall. The lizard hurtles through the air and I gasp, knowing the long drop on the other side, anticipating the crush of its body on the paving below. Tito rambles on, sees me in the window and salutes. I return a static wave then let my hand fall back to my side. The morning has collapsed; I need to get out, I need to walk.

There is no sign of the lizard outside the wall. I search up and down and am relieved not to find it. 'You landed safely, friend,' I say.

The Copacabana sand is cold when you dig your toes under its surface. I relish that cold; it brings to mind Nova Scotia and the antediluvian chill that place holds. I go to Great Village in my dreams and sit on Grandmother's lap and we chatter together, though I cannot hear the words. Those dreams make me lachrymose but they also bring peace – the profound joy of good memories works on me like balm.

I have the beach to myself and I push at hairy coconut husks with my feet to see if there is anything underneath. I scrabble in the sand for stones and shells. The ocean here does big work – the sand is powdery – so I rarely find anything unusual on my beach-combs. At home on my desk I have a treasury of sand dollars, lima bean stones and architecturally crosshatched Venus shells. This morning I find a wedge of green sea glass and it brings to mind Tito and his variegated eyes. The squally colour of the glass delights me and I pocket it.

I pass the huddle of beach shacks that sits up behind the tideline. They are made from driftwood and burlap sacks and even in winter they must swelter. Sometimes a boy sits outside the end shack. I say 'a boy' but he may be a man, it is hard to tell. He is retarded, this boy, his head is too small for his body, but he is beautiful because of it. This boy, with his long torso and tiny head, has a sweet, inquisitive face. '*Bom dia!*' I always call, with a wave of my hand, but he never replies.

I notice the smell of damp every time I re-enter our home. If there is such a thing as a national scent, then mildew is the smell of this land. Its moist fingers curl from the corners of every house and store and restaurant; a clay-like smell hovers everywhere.

'Lota, where are you?' I call out.

'In here,' she bellows, and I find her in the kitchen. She has already drunk the neck and shoulders off a bottle of whiskey. It is Irish whiskey – she claims Scotch tastes like tea. 'Top of the mornin' to you, Cookie,' Lota says, raising her tumbler.

'I doubt if Irish people actually speak that way.'

She grunts and shrugs. 'That new boy won't last.'

'Why's that, Lota?'

'Well, already he has you running from your desk, and I'm drinking and it's not yet noon.' She squints at the wall clock.

'None of that is his doing,' I say.

'There is also the problem of his idleness. I found him asleep under the coconut tree, stretched like a lord, farting and snoring.' I laugh, but Lota continues with her rant: 'I won't have it. He is lazy and we do not need another lazy boy.' She sallies on like this for a few more minutes, it being the Brazilian habit to keep explaining things – particularly uncomfortable things – long after the listener has understood.

I cut across her eventually. 'This week I have chosen to read not write,' I say, a plan that has just this moment occurred to me.

'Surely you have read the bookshelves dry,' Lota says, and plunges the cork back into the top of her whiskey bottle.

'Where is he now?' I ask.

'Who?'

'Tito,' I say, and she looks at me quizzically. 'The *boy*, Lota. The *boy*.'

'How should I know?'

I sit at my desk and read with dismay the lines I typed yesterday. Who was the woman who wrote them? And what foolishness made her believe they were worth a thing? I have been pulling and slapping the same poem into shape for months now and it will not behave. The words sit still on the page, logjammed. I poke my finger through the dish on my desk that is filled with my favourite shells and stones; the piece of green sea glass sits in its centre, winking at me. I snatch the sheet of paper from the typewriter and stuff it into the desk drawer. I will do what I told Lota I would do: I will read. I select a volume from the shelf – some friendly sonnets – and head for the yard.

Tito is kneeling on the path, bent over the bucket I gave him earlier, gazing into the surface of the water. I stand and watch him looking at his reflection like someone trying to find answers in the moon.

'Do you like what you see?' I ask. Tito startles. 'Your face. Do you find it handsome?' The boy jumps up and backs away from me. 'It's OK, Tito, I'm only making fun. Teasing.'

He closes his green eyes and purses his lips; he shakes his head, grabs the bucket and stomps off, water sloshing over his bare feet. His slender body retreats, rigid with annoyance, or embarrassment, or who-knows-what. I am beginning to wonder if Lota is right about Tito; if he will not last with us at all.

Sudden, blasting rainstorms are the order of August here; the sea and sky go from zinc to turquoise in the space of moments. The rain falls in televisual lines and clouds roll like demons along the horizon; the tide roars and complains. But when the storms end, the air is breathable and it is then I love to wander the beach to see if anything has been left for me.

Today I hope to find driftwood, lots of it. Tito has agreed to construct a bench to go in our yard and, for weeks now, he has been appearing with lengths of wood for my approval. I want to contribute some pieces too. This is our project, his and mine.

The sand is already dry by the time I walk it. Before long I spot a beauty: a stubby plank painted red with scatters of yellow showing through. I flop onto my knees to admire it, thrilled with its grain, its carnival colours. It will make a perfect armrest on the bench. I lift it and shake off the sand. From the corner of my eye I see someone approaching from the shacks above the tide line. But when I look up, ready to greet them, I see that they are not coming towards me at all, they are dancing. Outside the end shack, two people dance to a drumbeat, two young men. They roll their arms like windmills and dip their knees up and down; they shimmy around each other and kick their legs with solid grace. The drumbeat rises from a small girl who is beating out a rhythm on a tin can. I realise I recognise the young men, both of them: it is the retarded boy and it is Tito.

They dance on, circling each other fluidly as if this is something they have rehearsed. The girl's drumming gets wilder and the boys twist in a frenzy, their heads shaking voodoo style. In the end the rhythm is too crazed and they fall in a tangle of arms and legs onto the sand, laughing. I want to approach them but their joy is so intimate, so carefree, that I daren't break their spell. I take my piece of painted wood and lope on down the beach.

Tito is pleased with the piece of driftwood. '*Belíssimo*,' he says, rubbing his fingers over it, front and back.

'I saw you on the beach,' I say. 'You were dancing.'

'And I saw you,' Tito says. 'I see you often – gathering things.' He tilts his head and grins; he looks like a toddler when he smiles, which is seldom.

'I love that stretch of Copacabana,' I say. 'Is that where you're from?'

'I'm from Petrópolis, but I live on the beach with my brother.'

'You must miss the mountains, both of you.' I imagine a place where the air is thin and clouds clutch at peaks.

'We miss our mother,' he says.

For a moment, I am surprised by what he has said – I'm so used to the people here being occupied with the present and not things that can't be seen, like the past. But he is only a boy, of course, and he needs his mother.

'She's still there, in Petrópolis?' I ask.

'No, Miss. She is dead.'

I put my hand on his arm. 'My mother is dead too. We're the same.'

'No, Miss,' Tito says, gesturing at the garden, the house, the half-made bench. 'We will never be the same.'

'They are orphans, Lota. We must help.'

I have been building up, explaining, re-explaining, trying to be Brazilian in my approach, but Lota is unmoved. She puts her hands on my shoulders.

'Cookie, they are practically grown men. I wanted a boy to help around here. I did not want the full catastrophe.' Lota slips out of her slacks and tosses them into the hamper.

'They live in a hut covered with sacking. Did you hear me when I told you that? Don't you care?' Tears are starting to build and hurt my throat.

Lota shrugs and buttons up her pyjamas. 'I'm tired, Cookie, and I'm finished discussing this.'

She slides into our bed and turns her back to me. I stand over her, boiling and confused.

'For a woman of causes you surprise me. You're wounding me.'

Lota does not turn around and eventually I creep in beside her, but I hold my body rigidly away from her side of the bed.

In the rich geography of dreams, Great Village and Rio de Janeiro collide; winter in Brazil becomes a Nova Scotian summer and, in my grandparents' house, I am the old woman in the rocker and Tito is the child at my feet. I run my hands through his hair, soft as rabbit fur under my fingers; I croon a song to him. Outside the window, snow shrouds the beach.

I wake, grappling with this new reality, to find the bed empty beside me. Business has taken Lota away early; I will be alone for the day. A company of parrots raise their pandemonium in the yard and I listen to them argue back and forth before rising to go to my desk. I sit there and mull over how best to get Lota to help Tito and his brother. Perhaps if I spoil her a little, I will get my way; she responds well to devotion. We are a harlequin pair, for sure – Lota is mighty and spontaneous; I am naturally cautious. But we seem to fit, despite all.

Tito is out back, lining up pieces of wood for the seat of the bench; I watch him concentrate and configure. That he was mine in my dream has only increased my affection for him. He purses his lips, frowns, arranges the driftwood in patterns, then changes his mind and moves this piece here, that there. I go to the kitchen and stand by the door.

'*Bom dia*, Tito. Come have some iced maté with me.'

He hesitates but then joins me at the table and sits in silence while I prepare our drinks. Tito holds the straw delicately as he sips; his long fingers are stained and rough. I look at his face; the green eyes, the wet mouth. I still feel the dream softness of his hair under my hands; I feel like a grandmother, like a mother, like a lover. I smile at Tito.

'Miss?' he says.

'It's nothing, Tito. Nothing at all.'

I put my hand on his arm; he closes his over mine and squeezes. I let my lips fall to his fingers, kiss each one in turn. When I raise my head to gaze into his eyes, they are closed. Tito takes back his hand gently, stands and leaves the kitchen for the yard.

I put on a jazz record and prepare a supper of beans and rice with shortbread to follow. The candles I have placed here and there cast a cheery gloom. Lota comes in, all nerves, all light, chattering about what she has done for me, what she has done for Tito. I go to speak and she shushes me; she needs to get her words out before I can say a thing.

'I've found a position for him, with my old friend Gabriela in Petrópolis,' she says. 'She will be patient with Tito, being an idler herself. There is a small house on her land; he and his brother can live there.' She kisses my cheek. 'And when we build *our* house above Petrópolis, at Samambaia, maybe he can come work for us.' She stands and smiles, triumphant. 'There now, Cookie. I hope you are pleased.'

I take Lota in my arms just as a samba rhythm bursts from the record player; I spin her out in front of me and make windmills of my arms. Lota laughs and does the same. I dip my knees and she follows me. We shimmy around each other and kick our legs. Later, in our bed, I cup her small breasts in my hands and kiss her neck. Lota has a special heat; she is warm as Rio, warm as Paris, warm as Great Village on a high summer Sunday.

Tito and his brother come to say goodbye. They are polished and quiet in neat white shirts, alike despite the brother's rolling eyes, his too-small head. Tito holds his brother's hand, anchoring him to his side. Lota will drive them to the train and they will travel on alone to Petrópolis.

'I will miss you, Tito da Silva,' I say. 'I will miss your sweet face. Thank you for my bench. For everything.'

He nods and holds out his hand to me; lying in his palm is a piece of green sea glass, the match for the one I found on the beach. I take it from him and close my fist around it. I embrace Tito quickly and his brother lets a raucous squeal.

When they are gone, I go to the dish on my desk and take my own green sea glass from it. I pop it and the piece Tito gifted me into the breast pocket of my shirt. Now I carry Tito's eyes with me everywhere and my heart knocks against them in an eternal, maternal waltz: *babumf, babumf, babumf.*

Napoli *Abú*

Fuck knows how I ended up agreeing to go to Naples with a spinster. Not even *my* spinster but a stray of my sister's, offered up to me as a solution to my singlehood, a partner-in-the-pathetic.

'Beatrice is on her own too,' Clodagh said. 'She's into the kind of stuff you like – you know: art, old ruins, all that. She'd love to go to Italy.'

'I'm grand going on my own,' I said.

'Ah go on. Poor Beatrice is lonely, she could do with a break.'

So we sat side by side – two unbridled yokes – scrabbling for things to say, though the aeroplane hadn't yet reached ten thousand feet. Beatrice sneezed crazily as the plane climbed.

'Summer cold?' I asked, though I couldn't care less.

'Allergies.'

There's nothing I hate more than the allergy brigade with their I-can't-eat-this and I-can't-tolerate-that and 'does this have gluten?' Snot-spewed hankies in garlands around them. The only thing worse is a vegan. Jesus wept, I was surely headed into the longest week of my life. I fiddled with my iPod, thinking I could block her out with a consoling waft of Adele, but even

I knew that would come off rude. So I tried some conversation.

'Did you read about your man,' I said, 'who fried his wife's placenta and ate it?' Beatrice frowned and I noticed again the colander-shake of freckles across her cheeks, a waste on someone so plain. 'Or the fella who had liposuction and made soap from the fat? Lemon-scented soap. Imagine!'

'I heard a chap on the radio,' she said, 'who cooked his own hip and ate it. He said it tasted of goat.'

'Ah now, that's just mad, isn't it?'

I grinned at her, settled back in my seat and let the aeroplane's thrum wash through me. Beatrice mightn't be too bad after all. It could even turn out grand.

Beatrice didn't like Naples. It was too hot altogether, the people stared, the cobbles were too cobbly, the road works were overdone, and there was *way* too much graffiti for her liking.

'Who, Tara, would deface a thirteenth-century building? Just *who*?' She put her hand to the graffitied wall as if she might heal it. In Caffè Gambrinus she sipped at a latte and wasn't seduced by the pastries, though I would happily have eaten two. I ate a tooth-breaker of a biscotti instead, so she wouldn't think I was a pig, and cursed her with every bite. After an hour's worth of shopping, I suggested we leave the rush of Via Chiaia to walk the beach; she sloped glumly beside me.

'I hate sand,' she said, *sotto voce*.

Well, Beatrice, I wanted to say, in that case you can sit on a fucking towel on a bloody fucking bench. But there was something teachery – forceful – about Beatrice and I guessed I would neither swim nor sunbathe that day. Still, I tried.

'I *want* to go to the beach,' I said, meek as a newt in the face of her scowl.

Beatrice tutted and we trotted on, down towards the water, where even she was mesmerised by the sudden curl of the bay. We stopped to look from one end of the promenade to the other; a squat fort sat to our far left, oddly militaristic in the blur of boats and blue.

'The Bay of Naples. Lovely. I wonder what that is,' I said, indicating the fort.

'It's the Egg Castle. Castel dell'Ovo.'

'The Egg Castle? The giant womb, isn't that it? It was probably stuffed full of vestal virgins back in the day for the fellas to take their pick. Men, what?'

'You mean prostitutes, I suppose. Vestals took a vow of chastity.'

I snorted. 'Whatever. Do you think that kept the fellas off them? Men are all the same.'

'No, Tara,' she said, looking at me with those flat eyes, 'they're not.'

We strolled the promenade, though I ached for the lap of seawater on my toes. Before long we stopped at a restaurant for a pee; then we sat on the terrazza to have a drink – she had Orangina. Tee-bloody-total into the bargain, I thought. I started to tell her about Gabriel and, fair play to her, she listened to me banging on about how secretive he is, about the way he keeps everything to himself like some auld Fagin.

'I get fed up badgering for details about his life, so I go silent, but he doesn't seem to notice.' The wine made me tongue-waggy. 'I googled his wife, you know. She's a top-notch solicitor. Super successful. But square as all-get-out, ordinary. *Homey*. How did she ever turn Gabriel on? It's a fucking mystery to me. The first rule of shagging married men: never google the wife. Remember that, Beatrice, as you go about your business.'

I sipped my Falanghina and glanced at her: the helmet hair, the miniscule lips, the dour set to her face. Poor shite – what man would even look at her?

'My boyfriend is married too,' she said.

'You have a fella?' I sat up and leaned towards her. 'Seriously? A married man? Well, get you, the *capaillín dubh*.'

'I'm no dark horse, Tara. *You* expect people to be a certain way, that's all. Because of the way they look.'

She needled me with her cloudy eyes and I wasn't sure if she was referring to my comments about Gabriel's wife, or to herself. Whatever she meant, it shut me up. I drank my wine and looked out over the sea; the breakers were pearl-tipped and perfect, like waves in a film. The shoreline was spangled with semi-nude bodies, stock-still on towels, soaking up the frazzle. Oh to be flaked out beside them on a towel of my own. I looked back at Beatrice, who had remained silent.

'Go on, tell me about him,' I said. 'Did you google the wife?' Beatrice blushed scarlet. I smacked the table. 'You did, you mad thing!'

'I didn't need to. I know his wife.'

'Tut-tut, naughty-naughty, Beatrice, crapping on your own doorstep. That's worse than what I'm at – at least Gabriel is a work thing. No one knows anyone's other half in the office. Much better that way.'

'How is it worse or better or anything, Tara? We can care about it or not care about it, as we choose. I don't see that what I'm doing is good, bad or indifferent compared to your situation.'

'Ah, whatever. So who is he? Who is *she*?'

Beatrice fidgeted with the hem of her T-shirt; she sighed and looked out over the bay. I followed her gaze to the blue of the sea, the dark seam of the horizon, then turned back to her. She was studying her handbag now, as if it might hold the key to the universe; she started to root around inside it. Was she ignoring me on purpose? I was having none of that after her revelation and, after all, I'd fessed up about Gabriel to her.

'Well?' I said. 'Who is this Romeo?'

Beatrice dropped her bag to the ground, tossed her head forward and pulled a bandanna over her hair; she tied it at the nape of her neck. She wouldn't look at me.

'I'd rather not say,' she said eventually.

'Do *I* know him?'

She glanced at me, uneasy but cocky. 'You do.'

Who did we know in common? A few of the skins in Clodagh's group. Not a looker amongst them. Then a thought clattered me in the face.

'It's not Phelim is it?' I said. I snorted at the idea of anyone having an affair with my tub-tastic brother-in-law, but Beatrice had turned forty shades of puce. 'Jesus tonight! Listen, you're welcome to him.' I thought of

Clodagh suffering Phelim all these years and here was the bugger having an affair. With Beatrice, of all people! Mousy, miserable, boring-as-shite Beatrice. I stared at her and she looked back, calm as you like. Fuck it, they could have each other. What was it to me? I tipped the rest of the wine down my neck. 'Will we walk up to the castle?' I said.

'Sure.'

Castel dell'Ovo was long and flat-topped, punched with tiny windows; it sat in the sea on an island, as if it had risen from the water and anchored itself there.

'It doesn't look like an egg,' I said.

'It's not supposed to. They say Virgil put a magical egg into the foundations to hold the place up. If the shell got broken, the castle would collapse and Naples along with it.'

'Can you go in and look at the egg?' I said.

Beatrice reared her head back and gawped at me and, for the first time, she laughed. And she didn't just laugh she nearly puked up her Orangina she was gasping so much to catch her breath between guffaws. After each spasm she waved her hand and thumped her craw; she would look up at me for a second and burst again into hoots.

'For fuck's sake, Tara,' she said, between groans as her laughter died down. 'Oh my Lord.'

'What?' I said.

'God, Tara, you're gas. Did you not hear when I said the egg was magic? Bewitched!'

She giggled and set herself off into gales again. I like when people laugh – I'm a good-humoured kind of person and, even though I knew she was laughing at me, the mad sound of her was infectious and I was soon chortling too. We stood on the prom, a pair of Hiberno hyenas, barely able to stand for the gusts of laughter breaking through us. When we finally calmed ourselves, I linked Beatrice's arm and we sauntered on towards the castle.

'Ah, it's all crazy, isn't it, Bea?' I said.

'It is.'

'Men. Love. The whole shebang. You know, I keep getting spam in my email that says things like "Marriage is boring, affairs are fun". It's like the universe knows what I'm at and wants to annoy me.'

'But if it's not fun, why do you bother?' Beatrice said.

'I never said it *wasn't* fun.'

'You said Gabriel's wife is a successful solicitor. You seem threatened by the fact. Is that fun?'

I turned to her. 'Are you feeling threatened, now that I know you're trying to steal my sister's husband?'

'Steal him?' Beatrice laughed. 'What on earth would I *do* with him, Tara? I don't want to own Phelim.'

'No, I suppose not,' I said. 'Meanwhile I have no clue why I picked Gabriel to love, the most reticent man on the planet. But, there you go – I can't even do affairs right.'

'Do you love this Gabriel?'

'Ah, I suppose I do. Until the next one comes along.'

She broke away from me and turned to descend some steps that led to the beach; I followed her. I took off my sandals; the sand was talc-soft and hot under my soles. Beatrice kicked off her runners. We walked to the water's edge and let lacy waves wash over our feet.

'The first person we fall in love with shapes us, don't they?' Beatrice said.

'Is Phelim the only man you've ever loved?'

Beatrice shrugged. 'That first one moulds our idea of love, I think.'

'I bloody well hope not. My first was a self-focused manipulator. A redhead. Turned me off redsers forever.'

Beatrice pulled one foot through the water, watched its lazy arc. 'Do you ever think about family?' she said. 'Kids?'

'Brats? Gabriel says he'll give me a baby if I really want one. I'm hurtling towards forty. Not sure I need all that now.' I looked at her, the reflection of the Mediterranean made an angelic glimmer light her face. She smiled — one of those involuntary ones that slip up onto the lips because they can't be held down, a smile that's married to a secret. She looked luminous, standing there in the tide, a contented Madonna. A flash of childless Clodagh lit up my inner eye. 'Come here, Beatrice,' I said, 'you're not pregnant are you?'

'No, no. Not at all,' she said.

Her eyes were trained on the Castel dell'Ovo and she stared at that place as if all she knew or cared about would burst up from under its foundations and lay itself on the shifting waves before her, like some sort of answer to everything. Or maybe she expected an egg to rise up; a magical egg that could burrow deep inside and alter a life.

Tinnycross

By the time Oliver drove the avenue under the horse chestnuts, the bluebells were already thinning out. He had noticed puddles of cherry blossom along the pathways in the village. It struck some tender part of him that another year was spurting towards summer, leaving him in a muddled January place, trying to catch up. The house lay squat and crabby ahead, and Oliver could feel his mood switch to match it; the undulating angst that always accompanied him at Tinnycross began to roll through him. He was a young man again, suckled and strangled by the place, and at odds with every blade of grass on every acre of the land.

He pulled up in front of the house and sat for a while to quell his building rage. Oliver knew that like all such rages, his agitation was mixed with a kind of love. He often longed for Tinnycross – for home – for a version of it or for the past, but the place also repelled him. Wanting to be calm when he confronted Bunny, he sat in the car and waited, and willed himself peaceful.

After five minutes Oliver got out and went around the side of the house to the back door; the front door may as well have been welded shut it was used so seldom. He stepped into the kitchen and was assailed by an off-kilter brightness. And then by the sight of a woman standing at the table — his mother's deal table — kneading dough with care. She was silver haired, neat as an egg, and she — for it could only have been she — had reawakened the kitchen. His mother's furniture still stood: the table, the dresser, the chairs, but all of it looked glossy and fresh and the room's walls were painted. Things were immaculate again.

'You must be …' Oliver searched on his tongue for the right term. 'You must be the housekeeper,' he said, eventually, settling on that word because he could come up with no other.

'I'm Bunny's wife.' She threw a glance his way as if she had been expecting him.

'His wife?' Oliver said, and snorted. The woman stopped her kneading and stared at him. 'Is Bunny home?' he asked.

'He's below in the field. Will I ring his mobile?'

'No, I'll go down to him.'

She wiped her fingers on her apron and came towards him with one hand out. 'Fidelma,' she said.

'Oliver O'Donnell.'

She smiled. 'I know who *you* are.'

Oliver left the kitchen and stood in the yard. The land fell to the river — Tinnycross was one huge field with no ditches or fences to mark it out. Hay bales sheathed in black plastic were dotted around like giant cuts of liquorice, and a stand of rape burned its yellow among the green and brown. His heart swelled into his throat and he drew a few deep breaths. The familiarity of everything was both balm and thorn to him. It was quiet in the yard but he could hear the far off burr of a tractor. The bird calls were the same bird calls as forty years before and, God knows, forty years before that again. Oliver gazed down over the land. How could a field – one ordinary field – have such a pull on him?

He looked at his good brown shoes, then at the muddy track that led from the yard to the land. He should have put wellingtons into the car boot. He glanced back at the house, imagined the round of bread Fidelma would soon put into the range then set onto a wire rack to cool. Bunny's wife? Well. That surely changed things. By what luck had his brother, of all people, got himself a woman? Oliver shrugged and headed down the track, at first treading the verge to avoid the muck and save his shoes, then staying off the grass because of the sticky pearls of sheep shit littered like beads from a rosary. Bunny is a secretive quarehawk right enough, he thought.

Oliver looked up to find Bunny strolling towards him; he was a shambles as always in his torn fisherman's jumper and folded-down wellies. The wife's ministrations had extended only to the house, it seemed. Bunny was swinging a stick like a dandy.

'Olly,' he said.

'Bunny. How's the form?' They shook hands. 'And it's Oliver. Please.'

'So I don't get to be Bernard but you get to be Oliver. Big man Olly.' Bunny slapped the ground with his stick.

'Did you get my letter?' Oliver said.

'I got a letter from Folan and Company, if that's the one you mean.'

'We need to settle this, Bunny, for once and for all.'

Bunny whacked the tree beside him with his stick; it was the old hawthorn, bent sideways by the wind, its branches beseeching the tree beside it. That hawthorn was their mother's favourite tree. She would stand under its dense crown, hand to the trunk, and call daddy from the field for his meals and she didn't stray from it until she saw him coming towards her.

'There you are, Martin,' she'd say, as if he were an esteemed visitor, and they would walk together up to the house, to sit and eat and listen to the wireless.

Oliver looked at his brother, at the ferment of anger rising through him.

'We need to settle something, Olly, do we?' Bunny said. 'What's to settle?'

'Ah, don't start.' Oliver put his hands on his hips and stood in front of Bunny.

'You think you're the prodigal coming back here. Well, you'll get nothing out of me.'

'Bernard.' Bunny's wife had come down from the house without either of them noticing. They both looked at her. 'Why don't we go inside and talk?'

'It's none of your business, Fidelma,' Bunny said.

'Oh, I think you'll find that it is,' she replied.

She walked behind them up the track towards the house, a shepherdess herding a pair of recalcitrant rams.

Oliver stood in his parents' bedroom, watching dust waver in the air. Their marriage bed had become Bunny's. Oliver wondered whether the lousy shite had even bought his wife a new mattress. He recalled his father's last days in that bed. Daddy had started to say their mother's name again; it fluttered out of his mouth like a butterfly looking for somewhere to land. It sounded alien launching off his tongue: 'Catherine. Catherine. *Catherine.*' He hadn't called her by name for years; hadn't cajoled her, or pleaded, or thanked her with her given name. Their mother sat by the bed day after day, holding their father's hand, soothing him, wiping his drink-haunted face.

'It's all right, Daddy,' she said. 'I'm here, I'm here. Your Catherine is here. I'm right beside you, Martin.'

Mammy was gone now too – Oliver had not witnessed her death – but he could feel her in the house still, a revenant gliding from room to room. He put his hands on the cold iron of the footboard and gripped hard; he rocked himself and pushed his chin to his chest.

'Come through to the kitchen, Oliver.' Fidelma stood in the doorway; her voice was gentle. 'I've made tea. We'll talk.'

He didn't turn to look at her. 'Both Mammy and Daddy died in that bed.'

'I know that. Bernard told me.'

'I'm not trying to be cruel by saying it,' Oliver said, hanging his head. 'I just remember. This place makes me remember.'

'Memory is a true thing,' Fidelma said. 'But it can make fools of us too, slow us down.'

Oliver looked at her; he detected weights and troubles he knew nothing about and probably never would.

'This all ends with Bunny and me,' he said. 'No offence, Fidelma, but you won't be producing an heir. Tinnycross will go to God-knows-who.'

'Let's talk it out and see what we can come up with between us.'

Oliver followed her into the kitchen; Bunny had their father's seat at the side of the table near the range. If visitors ever deferred to Daddy, wanting him to take the head of the table, their father always said, with a serious glee, 'Wherever O'Donnell sits *is* the head of the table.'

Oliver said this to his brother, hoping to make him smile, but Bunny ignored the remark.

'We'll give you a third of the market value,' he said. 'There's the three of us in it now.'

'Mammy died during the boom, Bunny; I'm entitled to half of what it would have gone for then.'

'Are you trying to put me out of my home?' Bunny crashed his fist onto the table. 'Are you trying to kill me?'

'I only want what's mine.' Oliver rattled a teaspoon around his mug. 'My business has gone under. The bank is talking about repossessing my apartment.'

'Well, boo fucking hoo. If you can't look after yourself, it's no concern of ours.'

'Tinnycross belongs to both of us, Bunny. Mammy always said it. There's no way around that.'

'You took your time looking for your share.'

'I thought you'd give it to me and, then, well, you didn't.'

'And bankrupt myself? Are you fucking mad, Olly?'

Fidelma reached across and squeezed Bunny's arm. 'We have my money, love; the money from my house.'

'You want to give the man who killed my mother your money?'

Oliver stood. 'Ah, here, there's no need for that.'

Bunny dropped his head and spoke his words to the table. 'Mammy asked you to come to Tinnycross and you wouldn't come. She asked you again and again.'

'It wasn't that simple, Bunny, and you know it. I was in Dubai for Christ's sake.'

'Your mother begged you to come and you turned your back on her. You turned your back on Tinnycross.' Bunny pushed back his chair, stood and left the room.

'Not to worry, now,' Fidelma said, patting Oliver's arm.

'That was uncalled for. Bunny knows I was abroad, I couldn't get on a plane every time she asked me to come; she was always trying to get me home. I helped Mammy in other ways.'

'I know you did,' Fidelma said. 'Bunny is very attached to this place; we both are. He lashed out there and he shouldn't have.'

Oliver suffered a twist of jealousy – Bunny hadn't just landed himself a woman, but a decent, generous woman. A strong one who was happy with what she was made of; a woman secure in herself and the world.

Fidelma invited Oliver to stay the night. He didn't want to, but he couldn't leave everything undone either; he hesitated.

'Sure stay. Do,' she said. 'I'd be delighted to have you.'

'I will so,' Oliver said, and thanked her.

Fidelma made up his childhood bedroom. He could barely get himself across the threshold and into the bed, the room bulged with so many memories: days spent in sickness-induced fevers, nights spent in ones brought on by girls. At least the room smelled different now – he couldn't have stood it if it held the bitter whiff of his younger self.

Oliver lay rigid in the narrow bed below the window, watching the moon with her mouth agape, spilling light over Tinnycross. He could see the corner of the barn, lidded with corrugate and lit up by moon-glow. He felt the presence of his parents and was unsettled by the knowledge that through the wall his brother was in their bed with his wife. His noble, loving wife. Sleeping warmly beside her or, perhaps, complaining about Oliver in a low voice, cursing the only brother he had.

In the morning Fidelma propped a neat envelope against the milk jug that sat on the table in front of Oliver. He was breakfasting on his own; Bunny was already out on the land. Oliver picked it up, knowing without opening the flap that the cheque would have her signature on it, hers alone.

'Are you sure?' he said.

'I am. It's best to leave himself to me; I can deal with him. I'll sort it out.'

'Thanks a million, Fidelma,' Oliver said.

When he had finished eating he stood and shook her hand. Then he leaned in and kissed her cheek – awkwardly, shyly – and she pulled him close to her breast; he felt the warmth and goodness of her through that hug.

'Don't be a stranger,' Fidelma said, and she let him out the front door and waved him off as he drove away.

The plains around Tinnycross were green and dappled with sheep. Every other field held an inky lamb among its white brethren. This lamb was always a maverick, sitting or standing apart from the others, living its own quiet destiny. Oliver drove past and watched the lambs, willing the dark ones to gambol and play with the others, but they stayed where they were, resolutely alone.

Oliver thought about Tinnycross as he drove further and further away from it, on towards the city. He could feel the backward pull to its green and its yellow and its light. If only it were possible to be a child forever, to stay in that precious, pellucid place of scant worldly pain. But would he want it if he could have it? A return to boyhood and the gentle orbit of his parents. Bunny lording it over him. All the particular woes of youth, different to what the wider world offered but painful nonetheless. The car reached the motorway and he turned onto it, into the flow of lorries, buses and cars, all heading to the stacked unease of the city. Oliver knew he might never see Tinnycross again. He gripped the steering wheel and grunted, an attempt to quell the loss surging up through him. Is it possible, he wondered, to be in love with a field? One field set in a golden time that may, in truth, never have existed. And if it *is* possible, is it wise?

Fish

When you have seen your neighbour in the raw – and he has seen you seeing him – it cannot be undone.

You looked from your box room window down into Nicholas's garden but you didn't expect to see him standing on his puddled clothes, all chest-fuzz and stomach and genitals.

He stood, looking down at his shirt, jeans and boxers, then he lifted his eyes straight up to yours. Fuck. He swiped his hands together, looked at his palms and picked at them – pulling off fish scales, you guessed.

Half an hour earlier you had driven out of your estate, down the road, past the shops and onto the roundabout. There you saw Nicholas's lorry, on its side, spilling a sea of fish onto the tarmac. The fish were grey and doll-eyed and the road was completely blocked. Nicholas stood there among them, like a man from the Bible, with his hands outstretched. Some motorists were out of their cars, hanging around, watching. A taxi driver shouted at Nicholas, 'What the fuck?', then he got back into his cab and sulked. Nicholas threw himself onto the pile of fish and wailed. Then, he got up and walked away.

You followed him in your car, off the round-about, past the shops, up the road and into your estate, keeping to a near-impossible twenty kilometres an hour. Nicholas opened his front door and slammed it hard behind him. Slipping up your own stairs, you went into the box room and looked down into his garden. He had already stripped and you were full-frame in the window; his head lifted and you couldn't move. You saw his naked body and what fifty-three years had made of it. And he saw you seeing him.

So, you slipped your dress over your head, unhooked your bra and wiggled out of your knickers. And then Nicholas saw what forty-seven years had made of you – your skin, breasts and belly – and none of it could be undone. So you both smiled.

Futuretense®

'It's actually good that you're a foreign national,' Donncha said. He leaned back in his chair, hands behind his head, elbows splayed like wings. Cock-of-the-walk.

Maria smiled down at him; the smile hurt her cheekbones. 'For what reason?' she asked.

'The clients like it when the descriptions sound a bit broken-Englishy. It's sexy, you know?'

'But I'm Irish. I'm from Galway.'

Donncha snorted. 'Yeah, OK.' He shuffled papers on his desk and Maria dipped from foot to foot, weary of standing. 'Listen, when you're writing, think effervescent.' Donncha waggled his thick fingers. 'Think staccato.' His skin was the same mottled, churlish pink as a cow's udder; Maria wondered if it smelt of milk and dung. He swung in his chair and pulled himself to stand, his belly pouching forward, slack. 'Welcome aboard, yeah?'

Maria hoped he wouldn't try to shake her hand; his bovine fingers would be too much, too much altogether. She nodded at Donncha, lifted the basket of perfumes from his desk and carried it out of his office to her own. She sat and picked out a grenade-shaped bottle; she imagined throwing it at Donncha's temple and the nice thwack it would make as it hit flesh. Maria conjured the rainbow of bruises he would be left with, the welts and, eventually, the scabs. She twisted off the lid and sniffed deeply.

Terroriste® — Scent-bomb your territories with this explosive cocktail of masculine cyprus and wood, lashed to feminine frangipani. Terroriste® — for the woman who wants to be a man. Terroriste® — Forceful. Fragrant. Full on.

The office was in a warehouse in an industrial estate on the Naas Road. Maria had taken her flat in Fairview so as to be near the city centre; she wanted the throb of it close by. Now, every weekday, she went through the city on one bus and out past it on another, to a suburb on the far side. She left Dublin Bay at her back to enter the long, grey corridor of the town. Maria wondered about all the lives that went on in the apartments on the quays and the houses in Inchicore and Bluebell: the sex, the sorrow, the shame that filled those rooms, under lights and in darkness, seven days a week. But some of the people must be happy, she thought; they were bound to be, weren't they?

The buses she took chugged and stopped, stopped and chugged and, by the time she got off her last one for the day, it was late evening. The diesel smell of the buses reminded her of her father's New Holland, stinking up the boreen and the yard with its black fumes. Her mother called it 'that fucking yoke'; *her* family had always had Masseys, like *normal* people.

Maria would have to go west soon and show her face; she would have to endure her mother, complaining about her father and weeping into her apron over a dead calf or a vanished hen. The same woman who never dropped a tear at her own son's funeral.

HerStory® — Tonka bean and orange blossom vivify this homage to the female spirit. Childlike and luminous, HerStory's® vibrant top notes slide sensually above an earthy heart and silky accord. Tough and seductive, HerStory® is the new woman's fragrant manifesto. Wear it. Own it. Live it. HerStory®!

Dublin city unfurled before Maria at the weekends. Her mother had proclaimed it a foul place but Maria enjoyed the mix of oil and hops and exhaust-stink; she liked the moss-and-mud smell off the Liffey that was like no river in Galway. The buildings were various: a pagoda of glass floated above the Liffey; there were the columns of government, and soft red brick everywhere. Dublin's crowds energised Maria. She liked their push-me-pull, the endless spate of bodies and faces, everyone hurrying towards something and, later in the day, hurrying away from it.

'Dublin is awful depressing, Maria,' her mother said. 'And you can never tell what's what or who's who; the place is wedged with gutties. Keep yourself to yourself.'

Maria liked the southside of town as much as the northside. She spent Saturday afternoons strolling up and down Grafton Street to watch the whole clatter of life it held. She loved the flower-women with their rough faces. And the man who made a sand Labrador and stood over it all day, finessing its coat, as if the dog were real. Maria appreciated the buskers — the shy and the brazen – who tootled for the tourists on tin whistles and crooned in County America accents. She wondered if John had enjoyed the town when he lived in Dublin, or if London called to him from early on. Her brother had always wanted the next thing and the next; nothing in the now ever satisfied him.

John had worn a benign aftershave, remarkable only for its subtlety; Maria chose it for him though she was only a girl at the time.

'You can't wear Daddy's aftershave forever,' she said, standing behind John on the cold lino of the bathroom, watching him douse himself from the sailing ship adorned white flask, that reminded Maria of a baby's bottle.

'And what would you suggest, missy?'

'We'd have to go to Ballinasloe so I could show you.'

John drove her to the town in their mother's Fiesta, and he let eleven-year-old Maria sniff her way through every men's fragrance in every chemist's shop in Ballinasloe, until she found the right one. The scent she chose was called Futuretense and it came in a squat silver flacon. John had never heard of it but, when he sprayed it on, he told Maria it was the perfect one for him. He smelt his wrist and said, 'As comforting and elemental as a new lover.'

Maria grinned. She loved the way John spoke, like someone making up a poem on the spot. She was happy to be seen walking Society Street and Dunlo Street with him, proud to be his sister. John paid for the aftershave and they celebrated with tea and fairy cakes in the Bread Basket, and a breakneck spin back to Ahascragh in the Fiesta. John overtook every other car on the road and roared, 'Bogmen! Bogmen!' out the window as they sped by.

On one of Maria's wandering Saturdays, a man wearing Futuretense wafted past her and she swooned under its warm, woody scent; it brought her brother to her like a swift slap. She followed the man for a while, soaking up his trail of cyprus-tobacco-ginger, but she let him go once he crossed over into Stephen's Green. The moon was a yellow lantern rearing up behind the trees that rimmed the park; it was time for Maria to get back to Fairview and make her tea.

Luna Bella® – Unmask the urban emotion of Luna Bella®, an unprecedented mix of patchouli, leather and moon iris. Let your soul hover above its sophisticated intensity and be swept away on its urgent, ice-lily base. Everyone deserves the indulgence that is Luna Bella®.

'Cheer up; it might never happen,' the bus driver said.

Maria stood at the front of the bus, waiting to get off; the driver looked at her in the rear view mirror. She wanted to say, 'It already *has* happened.' But that brought too clear a picture of John, hanging in his London flat, his skin darkening as the days passed. So she smiled instead, into the mirror, before turning to look at the driver. He grinned back, showing two rows of bright, even teeth; Maria was always drawn to nice teeth.

The bus pulled in at her stop and the driver opened the doors. Maria stepped forward to alight but the driver closed the doors quickly before she could leave the bus. Maria turned to him again and he winked. He had choppy, fair hair like a footballer's. The bus driver was taking her in, noticing her as much as she was him.

'Ah, I'll stop messing now,' he said, pressing the button to open the doors. 'Go on. Cheerio.'

Maria thanked him and swung off the bus into the Fairview dark, bringing a small piece of the driver home with her. She savoured him as she ate her tea of tinned salmon and batch loaf; she sipped him up with her coffee. Later, in bed, his golden hair lay beside her on the pillow, smelling of sunflowers and honey and cognac, and Maria rubbed herself into ecstasy on his scent.

Tower de Nuit® – *Abandon yourself to the glamorous ride that is Tower de Nuit®, let it fill you with the lush, juicy undertones of star anise. Surrender to the joie de vivre of virile, glistening black orchid. Tower de Nuit®: Provocative. Risqué. Orgastic.*

Donncha stood over her desk; Maria had seen him lumber towards her. She held her breath; she did not want to smell him. He had that fat-person aura: a curdled, damp warmth that spoke of unwashed folds.

'Maria!' He blurted her name as if it embarrassed him to say it. 'Listen, I'm just thinking and, don't get me wrong, but you might want to tone it down a bit.' He wouldn't look at her, keeping his eyes instead on the print-out of Maria's work in his hand. She could see that he had yellowed-in parts of it with a highlighter. 'We're in the business of words, yeah? But "orgastic" – is that a

real word? What does it even mean? It sounds, you know,
rude maybe. What do you think?'

Maria placed the bottle of Tower de Nuit on the palm
of her hand. 'What does this look like to you, Donncha?'

'I don't know. The round tower at Glendalough?' He
squinted. 'A lighthouse? The Spire, maybe?'

Maria curled the fingers of her other hand around
the perfume bottle. 'And now?'

'Well, I can't really see it when you have your fist
around it like that.' He sputtered a laugh.

Maria moved her closed hand up and down the shaft
of the bottle. 'Now, Donncha? What does it remind you
of when I do that? Slowly, like this, then a little faster.
Oh!' Maria stilled her hand.

Donncha backed away, his face shining red as a
Sacred Heart lamp. 'Ah, yeah, I see what you're saying.
You're doing grand. Work away, work away.'

Maria watched him stumble over to the water
cooler; she listened to the glug of its innards as Donncha
helped himself to one cup of water after another. She
took out a perfume bottle from her basket and popped
off its lid.

*Ishka® – An aquatic interpretation of pure Irish water, Ishka®
flows from a top note of crisp green tea through to a base of
shamrock dew. Natural and earthy, the watery accords of this
fragrance's core tell of the man with an endless need for adventure. Ishka® – slakes every unquenchable thirst.*

The bus driver's name was Eddie Laharte. Maria knew
this because he had a totting-up sheet on a clipboard that

sat behind the steering wheel and, with her good eyes, she could read it. 'Maria has great eyes; brilliant eyesight,' was her mother's only boast about her as a child and, even then, it was as if she took credit for the fact.

John, of course, was beyond compare; there weren't enough superlatives for him. John of the top marks at school. John of the gobsmacking good looks – 'I don't know where he gets it from! But it's more than likely my side; the Uncle Jack was a fierce handsome man.' John of the thoughtfulness – 'He brings me breakfast in bed every Saturday; I kid you not, missus. He's a great lad altogether.' John of the lovely Ballinasloe girlfriend – 'She was Queen of the Fair last year!' John of the Dublin boyfriend. The Ahascragh girlfriend. Another Dublin boyfriend. Their mother couldn't keep up and, by the last boyfriend, she had lost any desire to try.

Eddie Laharte sang snatches of songs to Maria as he drove the bus, looking up at her from under his thatch of hair. He called her Roxanne and told her she didn't have to put on the red light or sell her body to the night. Maria liked his name. Eddie Laharte. In her mind she called him Steady Heart.

'So, Roxanne, what's your real name?' Eddie said and, when she told him it was Maria, he wondered how to solve a problem like her.

'You could take me out,' Maria said, appalled that the words of fantasy had fallen from her tongue.

'Grand so,' Eddie said, 'I will.'

And he ignored the complaints of the other passengers while he stopped the bus on the North Strand

and took his time swapping mobile phone numbers
with Maria.

*Cherrybomb® – Bold but with a soupçon of lux, Cherrybomb®
is a candied, berry surprise. The top, heart and base notes of
the fragrance sing to the innocence of the young while anticipating the mature yet vibrant accents of cerise and vanille.
Cherrybomb® – the rubescent scent of youth, just waiting to
be plucked.*

Maria was summoned west. Her mother met her off the
train in Ballinasloe.

'He's taken to the bed,' she said, as she swung the car
out into the road and turned left towards Ahascragh.

'Daddy?'

'Of course Daddy. Who else is there? He's asking for
you morning, noon and night.'

Maria looked at the houses they passed; some neat
and cared for, others with crumbling stone walls and
broken windows. The next house along, she knew, had
a Virgin shrine at the bottom of its garden; Mary standing with pleading arms and a let-down look. Blessed
Mother of Ballinasloe. Virgin of Ahascragh. Mother of
Sorrows. Our Lady of Suicides. Sancta Maria. Pray for
us.

'I have bad news,' her mother said.

Maria looked at her. 'Oh God. Is he very sick?'

'Is who sick?'

'Daddy.'

Her mother jammed her foot to the brake and Maria
jolted forward. 'Not him! The dog! The dog died. Boy

– John's old pal.'

Her mother started to whimper and Maria told her to pull over; she parked beside the house with the shrine. The Madonna's halo of bulbs sparkled in the dusk, a sapphire torc; Maria was enchanted by the blue glow and only gradually became aware of the sustained sobbing beside her. She switched on the map light and saw that her mother's face was flooded with snot and tears.

'Here you go.' Maria handed her a tissue from her bag; it was a dusty lump that held a portion of the gallons of tears she had leaked over the loss of John.

'You'll have to bury Boy,' her mother said. 'With himself in the bed, I can't manage the digging of the grave, the lifting, all that. Poor Boy, he was a terror but I loved him. Who will I have left?' Her mother pushed out another few tears and dabbed at her eyes.

'I'll drive,' Maria said.

They picked their way over cow pats to get to the place by the horse chestnuts where the pets were buried over the years; there were crosses for gerbils, dogs, cats, goldfish and Maria's beloved pet duck, Bernie. Maria wore a pair of wellies that may have been hers or may have been John's, she wasn't sure; they felt dank on her feet.

'Do you remember, Mam, you used to heat up the insides of Daddy's wellies with the hairdryer before he went out in the mornings?'

'What? Not at all. I did no such thing.'

Maria looked back up at the house, standing like a headstone on the hill; geese squabbled around the pond in the low field. How had Maria never noticed before that the pond was heart-shaped? A deep, steady heart. She wondered if Eddie would send her a text while she was at home and, if he did, what it would say.

When they reached the spot her mother had chosen to bury Boy, Maria began to dig. The peaty, wormy clay threw up the smell of childhood to her nose. She and John had spent hours in these fields, digging to Australia and making Sindy doll graveyards. Maria began to enjoy the cleave of the shovel through the quaggy earth, the primordial feel of it. She moved the clods quickly and felt as if John was beside her, helping to open the ground, sure now that he wanted a Galway burial and not the ash-scatter on the Thames of his note.

Her mother sat on the grass, holding the swaddled Boy to her chest. She dipped her face close to the bundle of him and sighed. Maria worried that she might kiss the old sheet that covered the dog. Or worse, unwrap him and put her lips to his coat. She kept digging. Boy was a squat terrier and it did not take long to fashion a big enough hole, or fill it in above him. They stood over the grave. Her mother's eyes were closed and Maria hoped she was not going to recite the Rosary or anything like that.

'He was the needle in my compass,' her mother said.

The trees rustled and Maria watched a chestnut drop to the earth and split.

'He was a lovely little dog, all right.'

Her mother's eyes sprung open. 'What are you saying? Not Boy! John! John! Sure I'm lost without him. Lost. And your father is useless to me. The whole thing has fallen asunder.'

K9® – Make a statement with quirky K9®! The Irish Setter-shaped flasque will be a favourite talking point. Loyal and fresh, with a blend of emerald grass and bright satsuma, K9® is a strong balance of the classic and the modern. K9® – rugged, faithful, true.

The bus was wedged with people as it always was in the evenings. Eddie was not the driver and Maria worried that by going west she had upset some equilibrium, knocked things skew-ways. She left Eddie driving the bus on Friday – he was there, safely there where he should be – but now he was no longer behind the wheel. There was a man with onyx skin in his seat.

'Where is Eddie Laharte?' Maria asked the driver, put out that this man was at *her* man's wheel. He shrugged and shook his head.

Maria sat. The young fella sitting in front of her had lipstick on his cheek, a perfect pink pout; the girl beside him eyed it manically. A teenager across the aisle had blood dripping from no discernible wound on her ear and it tattooed her collar. Maria wanted to tell her; she would like to tamp the blood for the girl but could find no way to say it, so she said nothing. The elderly man who sat beside Maria talked about Blackhall Place and Fitzwilliam Square and the women who roamed those places.

'It's all gone on the internet now,' he said, 'all *that*.' He licked his lips and caught her eye. 'Isn't that right?'

'Maybe,' Maria said, looking out of the bus to see an aeroplane leave its scribble across the sky.

She thought of her father, how small and vulnerable he had looked in her parents' bed, with his hair tossed into a silver peak. The room smelt, as it always did, of mildew and soup.

'Hello, Daddy,' she had said, an offering from the doorway of the bedroom.

'Maria! Thanks be to God. Get in and close that door. I haven't got long; your mother is killing us off one at a time: first John, then Boy. She's after me now. I needed to warn you.'

'John hung himself, Daddy. And Boy ran under the wheels of the New Holland, didn't he?'

'Is that what she's telling people? The fucking witch. She strangled the pair of them with her hands. I saw her.' Her father gripped Maria's arm. 'Listen, 'til I tell you. Stay away from this house. Stay away from Ahascragh. Settle yourself well in Dublin and don't be coming back here at all.' He glanced at the closed bedroom door and lowered his voice. 'She's threatening to put me into Brigid's in Ballinasloe. *She's* the madwoman and she wants to shove me into that place full of gombeens and nutjobs. If she doesn't squeeze the life out of me first.' He whispered: 'Stay away or you'll be next.'

Le Fou® — Experimental rose, combined with edgy accents of sambac jasmine, lift the wearer of this scent into new realms. The skin tingles under the powdery warmth of Le Fou's® exceptional heat, and pink peppercorn adds a sparkling facet. Le Fou® — Kooky. Exciting. Fantastical.

Eddie brought Maria for a picnic in the Phoenix Park. They sat on a bench and he took cheddar sandwiches from a Tesco cool bag. They both decorated the cheese with Tayto and crunched through the sandwiches under the eye of the Wellington Monument that rose up from the grass like God.

Eddie handed her a Double Decker. 'Bus chocolate,' he said, and they both laughed.

When they finished eating, Eddie stood and suggested a walk. He put his arm around Maria's shoulder and they strolled deep into the park, into the wooded, quiet part. The smells were welcome to Maria: the pinch-cool air of autumn, muck, grass and Eddie's warm, masculine fug – a mix of sweat and cheap deodorant. He took a small rug from his Tesco bag and they sat on it, their ears full with the friendly sounds of the park: the burr of distant cars, leaf-loss from the trees and murmurs from the living earth.

Eddie tilted Maria's chin and she watched his golden fringe fall over his eyes as he closed them and leaned in to kiss her. He tasted not of crisps or chocolate but of something sweet and rosy, something like hope. Maria let her tongue slip over and around Eddie's. Soon all there was in the world were their two mouths and their meet, tease, and delight in the soft heat of the other. When they broke away, Eddie smiled and Maria felt a lurch from groin to throat. He pushed her back gently so that she was lying down and he lay beside her.

Maria looked up at the sky. 'My brother topped himself in January,' she said.

'My little brother drove his car into a wall. We don't know if he did it on purpose or not.'

'The Dead Brothers Club.'

'I know a few more in that,' Eddie said.

'Me too.'

Eddie took her hand and they both closed their eyes. The park hummed around them, keeping up a hushed banter while they dozed. When Maria woke she saw a pair of fallow deer standing a few steps away, the stag's antlers poised like question marks, the doe's jaw working on grass.

'Eddie,' she whispered, nudging him.

He opened his eyes, hunkered into his standing and helped Maria to her feet. They picked up their things and backed away from the deer. The stag nodded his head as if in blessing and the doe kept up a rhythmic chewing and stared at them from succulent eyes.

Herne du Bois® – *A strong base of oriental musk coupled with oak-moss makes Herne du Bois® a deep yet soaring scent for the discerning man. Smoke fuses with green chypre in the base notes creating an earthy, masculine body. Herne du Bois® – taming the wild.*

Maria sat at her desk, feeling suddenly slick all over; sweat pushed between her breasts and slid inside her thighs. It was her body remembering – before her mind caught up – the sex she and Eddie had had that morning. He lay over her and held her gaze and his tongue lifted behind his teeth as he moved. He had sleep scars on his cheek, as if his skin had been folded and refolded. Maria recalled his low grunts when he rocked over her, and the final, giddy fall to her neck, and the way he kissed the skin there in small, picking kisses. She conjured the soft wet of his tongue; remembered the astounding tenderness of him.

'Erm, there's someone here to see you.' Donncha stood in front of Maria's desk; she hadn't heard him approach.

'Someone for me?' She rose and looked behind Donncha. Her mother stood there, alien and uncertain in the middle of the floor, her dark coat making a jackdaw of her. 'Mammy?'

Maria went and put her arms around her mother, breathing deep on her grease-and-sherry scent.

'I'm sorry, peteen; I had to get away from your father. He's raving. I hopped on the train.'

Donncha stepped forward. 'You can use the canteen to talk, yeah? Get yourselves a cup of tea.'

Maria nodded her thanks and steered her mother towards the door. She sat her in a chair and knelt beside her.

'He's saying John is better off dead.'

'Daddy doesn't mean that, Mam. He was mad about John.'

'How can he say it then?'

'I suppose he's hurting still and doesn't understand.'

'I'm afraid of my life of him. He half-choked me this morning and I ran from the place.' She put her hand to her neck.

'You can stay with me tonight, Mammy. We'll go to Ahascragh in the morning and see what's what.'

Donncha urged Maria to go home and she thanked him and bundled her mother to the bus stop.

'I don't know what to do with your father at all. As if I haven't enough to be dealing with.'

Maria leaned into her mother's side and tucked stray hairs behind her ear. 'It'll be all right, Mam, we'll get Daddy sorted. You'll be OK too. We have to stop looking behind us now and start looking ahead.'

Her mother nodded and patted her hand. 'You're a good girl, Maria, a great girl. You always were.'

They sat with arms linked on the bus into town, her mother stiff at first, as countrywomen always are in the face of Dublin's grime and hustle. But Maria could feel her mother's body slacken as the bus trundled on past the canal where swans performed their watery skirr.

When they stepped onto the Fairview bus, Eddie said, 'Hello, honey.' Maria smiled and indicated her mother, hooshing her into a seat near the front.

'They're a bit familiar these Dublin bus drivers,' her mother said.

Maria turned to face her. 'Actually, he's not just the driver. He's my boyfriend.'

'He is not!' Her mother leaned off her seat, into the aisle, to get a look at Eddie. 'What's he called so?'

'Eddie. Eddie Laharte.'

'Laharte? Is that some kind of came-over-with-Cromwell name?'

'I don't think so. His people are from Kilkenny.'

'Oh,' her mother said, nodding. 'Eddie Laharte.' She tested and re-tested the shape of the words on her tongue. 'Eddie Laharte.' Finding them pleasing, she settled back in her seat and grinned approvingly at Maria. They both fixed their eyes forward to the front of the bus, to where Eddie sat, whisking them onwards to Fairview and the future.

Futuretense® – *A light top gives way to deep, steady heart notes that seductively lead to a harmony of relaxing tobacco and warm ginger. This is a fragrance that thrusts its wearer forth into unknown realms. Futuretense® – promise in a bottle. Futuretense® – the only way forward.*

Squidinky

Brine gets into your blood when you live beside the sea; it gets into your bones. You flow with a watery energy that carries you along. But you can become tough and unwieldy too, like salt-cured fish. I haven't always been a shore dweller but ending up here with Luke made me feel at peace. I live above Squidinky, my tattoo parlour, and at night I hear the sea shushing and the tourists who patter by, drunk on beer and each other.

Lying in bed I pluck sleep crystals from my eyes, stretch until my bones click, then heave myself up because my bladder is leading me to the bathroom. To my daily surprise the mirror above the sink tells me that I am old. Hovering in front of it I examine my shirred jowls and the yellow tinge to the waterlines of my eyes.

'Not too bad,' I announce, because if I say it enough it might be so.

Sunny days clang here: children beat buckets with spades, the ice cream van tinkles 'O Sole Mio', and parents whine and smile. There is such pleasure in letting all life take place outside my window, to those who come to the sea in search of happiness and escape. They are right to come here. This is the home of happy.

I won't open Squidinky today; the skins of a few more people can stay blank until tomorrow – things are slow in the spring anyway. This is a day for walking and relaxing; for air in the throat. After my porridge, I wrap my slacks into my socks and pull on rubber boots. Luke's green cape coat will keep me cocooned if the wind is high.

Outside, the town is morning quiet and there's a tang of fish-rot. I head along Walk and Run Avenue to the top of the terraces, planning to end up at the pebble beach. I pass the ghost hotel that sits on one wing of the town; there's a ghost estate on the other. Refugees from Nigeria and Ivory Coast used to live in the hotel but they are gone now, taking with them their turbans and kaftans, their firm-faced children. They had a church service above the Spar every weekend and it oozed joy: they sang and clapped and shouted. I often stood outside to soak it in after buying my few messages. The people were moved, I think, to the direct provision centre in Athlone and, no doubt, they are the worse for it.

I continue along the avenue; pansies planted along the tops of stone walls curl their faces away from me like shy babies. I have the streets to myself and I savour the slap-and-echo of the soles of my boots on the footpath. The avenue feels long today but not in a bad way; it is uncluttered except for parked cars. I always relish that feeling of being queen of the town when I take an early walk. The sea glints through the gaps in the houses and I glance at it, anticipating the soothe of its blue expanse when I get to the beach.

The bench above the strand is occupied and I am put out. Who is this sitting on my seat? As I draw nearer, I see that the man on the bench is wearing socks and sandals. The first thing I always look at is people's shoes, don't ask me why. Socks and sandals, of all things. The man turns to me and raises his hand.

'Hello!' he shouts, as if we are friends. I nod and go to take the steps down onto the beach but he pats the bench. 'Sit, sit. Come and take a seat here. Look at the view!' He tosses his hand at the bay as if he owns it.

'I'll sit for a minute,' I say.

This *is* my bench. Well, it's Luke's bench; I put it here for him after he died, replacing a wooden one with fraying slats. On a cold day it is not as warm as the old seat but the Council said steel would weather better. I am possessive about this bench, about its position overlooking the bay and the two lighthouses – Luke's favourite view. I sit at the opposite end to the man and stare out to sea. A messy cloud, like the aftermath of an explosion, hangs over the horizon.

'If you just looked at that little slice,' the man says, making a frame around the cloud with his fingers, 'you'd think all was not well.' He lowers his hands. 'But of course, all *is* well.' He looks at me, his worn face alive with smiles.

'Is it?' I say. 'What about the economy? Bankers? The hospitals?'

'What about the here and now?' he says.

A young mother in pink runners barrels past with a three-wheeled pram; she pushes her sunglasses up on her head. Her child, a portly toddler, looks backwards, up at the mother, and does the same.

'Sunglasses on a baby,' the man says, 'isn't it marvellous?' He rummages in a plastic bag at his feet. While he is distracted, I stand up. 'Have some fruit!' He hands me a red apple. 'It's a Jonaprince.'

I take the apple. 'Thank you,' I say and trot away.

He shouts, 'Cheerio!'

The man has tumbled my walk from its natural path and now I have to continue on into the marram grass and pretend that I don't mind. Soon I am tripping over the things the sea has belched up: barrels, lager cans, a wooden pallet. I stop walking and pull wind into my lungs then let it out. Ducks in chevron flight skim over my head and I watch them until they disappear. I veer down towards the beach where oystercatchers poke about in the sand.

In the ladies bathing shelter, I sit and look at the apple. I feel like tossing it away but instead I polish it with the hem of Luke's coat and bite into it. The skin is bitter so I eat the flesh and spit the peels onto the ground. Luke's voice floats into my head: 'Spitting women and crowing hens will surely come to some bad ends.'

He always said that and I always answered, 'It's *whistling* women not spitting women.' Luke would shrug and we'd both smile. One of our shared rites.

I cannot even put a name on the feeling of missing Luke – it's too raw, too wide. All I know is that I am alone in a waiting room and the world has receded. My heart opens and closes like a mouth that wants to speak but can't form the words. The days carry forward in regular ways – I ink people, I eat, I watch television documentaries – but I push myself through weeks with a strength that seems to belong to somebody else. Mourning is hard work, it is long work; every twenty-four hours is a new lesson in learning the proper way to grieve. It's as though I am swimming through seaweed and just as the water begins to clear I whack into the hull of a boat.

I throw the apple butt onto the beach and the oystercatchers scatter then regroup. The rocks below the shelter are decorated with doughnuts of amber lichen; they bring colour to the grey. Between the rocks, shell caches lie in sandpits – mussels and winkles, empty of meat. I heave myself up and exit the bathing shelter. The man is still at Luke's bench but now he is standing. I take a wide arc to avoid him. He will think I'm rude but, sure, let him off.

'Ahoy!' he shouts, waving his arms like someone signalling from the deck of a ship.

'Jesus Christ.' I throw my eyes up in apology to Stella Maris who watches over the harbour from her plinth.

'Missus,' the man shouts, 'wait!' He putters up beside me. 'I'll walk with you.'

'I prefer to keep my own pace.'

'Not at all,' he says. 'You have "lonely" bobbing like a balloon over your head.'

I tut but he is undeterred. He comes with me, his plastic bag swinging at his side, all the way down Walk and Run Avenue to my door. We don't speak and I feel foolish and annoyed; foolish for being irritated – what harm is he doing? – but annoyed with him too for this disruption to my morning.

'Now,' I say, 'I'm home.' I fish my key from the coat's deep pocket.

'"Squidinky",' he says, craning to look at the shop sign. 'Well, if that doesn't beat all.' He sticks out his hand and I take it; he closes his other hand over mine and I see his knuckles are dotted with ink. 'Have a lovely day now, missus. Be good to yourself.'

Once inside the quiet of my hallway I feel I should be pleased as a peashooter to be on my own again, away from the pestering man, but I'm not. I am disarranged. I unpeel myself from Luke's coat and pop it onto its hook. It hangs like a collapsed cross and I twist it to press my face into the lining, searching for a whiff of him, the smallest scent. There is nothing there.

Luke would disapprove of all the time I spend alone now. It was he who kept up the friendships while I looked after the business. And because he was the one who rang people, who invited, greeted and mollycoddled them, after he was gone, I was forgotten. Our friends were his friends, it turned out.

In the morning 'O Sole Mio' drifts into my half-sleep. I think it is the ice cream van come a season early but it's someone whistling. The whistler trills the rising notes of the tune and drags them out; the sound is sweet wafting up to my bedroom. The words sing themselves in my head: *Che bella cosa na giornata 'e sole.* What a beautiful thing is a sunny day.

I peep out the window and see the man from Luke's bench standing outside. Gulls lunge around him, their cacophony hardly keeping up with their bawling beaks. The man whistles louder to drown them out, then throws his arms up in surrender. He laughs.

When I open the door to the parlour he is still out-side.

'Hungry,' the man says, and I'm not sure if he is refer-ring to himself, me or the gulls.

'Can I help you?' I ask.

'I think so. I want to get a tattoo covered up.'

'Your knuckles?'

'No, no,' he says. 'Can I come in?'

I stand back and he walks past me, the same plastic bag rustling in his hand.

He takes a seat, removes his jacket and unbuttons his shirt. His story is revealed: he has been seaman, lover, convict. His chest is hairless and the nipples are two oxblood coins.

'So which one do you want covered?' I say, taking in the blurred lines of mermaids, and Sailor Jerry pin-ups, the lexicon of names: Mabel, Assoulina, Grace.

He stands and looks in the mirror, pushes his shoul-ders back to right the sag of his skin. 'Do you know what?' he says. 'Give me a new one altogether.'

I haul a book of flash from the counter for him to look through. 'Where do you want to place the new piece?' I say, my juices up at the idea of giving him something to blend with the cascade of ink on his chest. I hold out the book. 'Here you go.'

He puts his hands behind his back, refusing to take it. 'I don't want some readymade thing. I trust you.' He sits again, whistles a bar of 'O Sole Mio' and looks up at me.

'You trust me? You don't know me.'

'I know enough.' He slips off his shirt and shows his back to me; there are no tattoos. 'There's a man in

Catalunya who collects tattooed skins. He says he'll buy mine when I'm done with it.'

'That's big in Japan,' I say. 'Well, maybe not big but they do it there.'

'I've been saving my back until I met the right artist. I want the sun – a great furze and orange ball of light. I want it to have a face.'

'I can do that.'

'I know you can. Like I said, I trust you.'

He comes every day after that and I work on his back; the sun's rays lick at his shoulder blades and armpits; its face frowns on the right side and smiles on the left. He asks me to put bones across the eyelids and a skull on each cheek.

'Everything has light and dark,' he says, 'even the sun. We'd be as well to keep that in mind as we go about our lives.'

My machine buzzes and he talks and talks. About his days as a seaman, about life in the belly of a ship. He tells me that Barcelona was his favourite port and how he misses the unpredictability of an onboard existence; the ferment of the uncertain.

I mention Luke, little snippets: our trips to India; his love of musicals, especially when Esther Williams was involved.

'It gave him such pleasure to watch that Esther swim,' I say. 'Luke was a merman, most at home around, in or on water. He taught me to love the sea.'

'I'm that way myself, half human, half fish,' the man says. 'You miss him, your Luke.'

'I do, of course.'

'How long?'

'A couple of years, nearly three.'

'Are you ready to let him go?'

Am I? This I don't know. I dip my needle and shade one of the skulls in the design on his back; it's benign, more Day of the Dead than Grim Reaper. Blood bubbles through the skin and I pat it away. *Will* I ever let Luke go? Do I have to? The absolute shock of his loss has eased, of course. That paroxysm that grief drags you down into swallowed me for the fat end of eighteen months. But I rose out of its depths somehow and found a plateau where I can exist, even if it is in a melancholic trance. I am lonely, it's true, but it's more than that – I'm alone.

I lift my finger off the machine and the room is quiet. 'I don't think you let go of the dead, exactly,' I say. 'You just place them into one of your heart chambers and open the door every so often. To invite them out.'

The man pushes himself up on his elbows and turns his head to face me. He nods and smiles and I am surprised to see his eyes are brimming, about to spill. He sits up and I hand him a tissue; I watch while he dabs at his face and lets whatever sadness has surfaced gust through him. It emerges on long sighs and cascades of tears.

'Are you all right?'

'Why don't we call it a day for today?' he says.

'If you're sure? All I've done is a bit of shading.'

'Let's go out for a walk. See what's to be seen.' He snuffles, blows his nose and exhales, vaporising whatever those thoughts were that upset him.

'A bit of air might do us both good, a little time out,' I say, peeling off my blue gloves and dropping them into the bin.

'Haven't we all the time in the world, the two of us?'

He sits up on the side of the tattoo couch and I wash him down with cold water and rub emollient into his skin. I watch him put on his shirt; he does it deliberately, with care, unlike Luke who made a hurry of every small thing. I catch the scent of lemon off his clothes, that sweet freshness that always makes me feel hopeful and at ease.

We lock up the parlour and head along Walk and Run Avenue to the top of the terraces, past the ghost hotel and along the stretch where the residents have planted flowers on the tops of the stone walls. There are daffodils now, sweet and smoky and bright as the sun. We stop to sniff them and smile at each other, our noses bent into the flowers' yellow bells.

Once at the beach, we sit on Luke's bench and look out over the bay and the two lighthouses. Stella Maris watches over the water and the boats, her arms raised in an eternal blessing. I take my new friend's hand in mine and he throws his other arm around my shoulder; I lean my head against his head, feel the heat from his skin. He whistles a few bars of 'O Sole Mio'.

'Brine gets into your blood when you live beside the sea,' he says. 'It gets into your bones.'

We sit on, watching the oystercatchers and the ducks, the swoon of the marram grass. The bench grows warm beneath us. And the sea sways and shimmers under the awakened glow of a March sun.

Men of Destiny

after Jack B. Yeats

July, with its pressing light, its high note of optimism, was ending. Storms came easier day by day and one roiled up now from the horizon with great cauliflower clouds and a bouncing wind. Patrick skelped from one side of the pier to the other until the boat docked, then he fell in beside Malachy who tore up the pier like a man on fire.

'No catch?' Patrick said.

'There were mackerel out by Mullaghmore, but I left them be.'

'Why so?' said Patrick, juicing for the truth from Malachy's own lips.

Malachy stopped and stared at his nephew. 'Stop following me. Go home where it's safe.'

'I won't,' said Patrick. 'You'll be glad of me by and by.'

Malachy ran towards the hill, dodging over walls, hoping to lose Patrick. He's a conundrum, Malachy thought, a fool of a lad. He slipped behind Aggie's cottage and watched Patrick sail past on his bicycle. Malachy waited below the house until the sun was swallowed up by the sea, then he slunk through Aggie's gate, back down to the pier.

He rapped on the hull, three knocks followed by three more; he heard the answering whistle and leapt onto the deck. The hatch opened and Malachy slid through; the stench of sweat hung in a rich fog, mingling with the fish-gut smell that he was used to. The men were sitting on the boxes, rocking with the movement of the boat.

'We'll wait for the storm to get up and then we'll move,' Malachy said. The men nodded.

Walsh turned to Malachy. 'Did you hear what they're saying Pearse said? "The only thing more ridiculous than an Ulsterman with a rifle is a Nationalist without one".'

Malachy looked hard at Walsh then he laughed; the others, then, were free to laugh too. Outside the wind gusted and moaned, lifting waves under the boat that made it judder from stern to bow. But still it didn't rain.

'Jesus, what's keeping it?' Malachy said. He looked at the others. 'A Sligoman praying for rain, hah?'

The men laughed again then sat in silence and smoked, lighting one cigarette off the butt of the last. The boat swooned high and higher, then jolted downwards, making the others look like heaving puppets to Malachy. Eventually the rain began to pelt and, when it was thundering onto both port and starboard, Malachy gave the signal. The men squashed their cigarettes and Walsh opened the hatch and climbed out. They passed the boxes hand over hand to the deck, then each of them crawled up, keeping their heads low.

Walsh stood on the pier and whistled; Aggie stepped into view and nodded. The rain thrashed and the wind sang. They carried the boxes up to Aggie's cottage, jemmying them open with a crowbar on her tidy mud floor. Aggie threw the splintered wood from the boxes into her fire and watched it blaze. The men loaded the guns into the coffin Aggie had made especially for tonight and she sealed it shut, the same way she closed the lid after every village wake.

She stood by Malachy and whispered the names of the townlands to him: 'Ballinagallagh, Cashelgarran, Gortarowey, Lisnalurg, Cregg, Kilsellagh.'

He repeated them back to her. 'Ballinagallagh, Cashelgarran, Gortarowey, Lisnalurg, Cregg, Kilsellagh.'

'Always have a name ready on your tongue, Malachy. Say it surely, like you know it as well as your hands. God speed, son.' Aggie made the sign of the cross on his chest and pushed him out the door.

The men lifted the coffin onto the cart. Walsh, the slightest, was dressed in Aggie's old shawl and skirt. The men flanked him and they each put a hand to the cart and pushed, heads bent against the storm.

By Barnaderg Malachy's feet were bleeding. By Mullaghnaneane he was cursing himself for thinking this could be done at all. He heard a low whistle and raised his hand. The men stopped the cart. A figure stood out on the road ahead; the man came forward, his uniform soaked to a dull grey.

'Whose funeral is this?' the soldier said.

'It's James Walsh's, sir,' Malachy said. 'The consumption took him two days ago.'

'James Walsh? Of what townland?'

'Gortarowey.'

'And who are you?'

'His brothers,' Malachy said, 'and his wife.' He indicated Walsh who kept his chin tucked down and his hand to the knot of the shawl Aggie had draped over his head. 'We're making for Drumcliff.'

'That's a long journey on a night like this,' the soldier said.

'It is, sir, but we dare not leave the body at home. For fear of the disease.' Malachy could feel his jaw working oddly. His voice sounded steady but his mouth pulled against the saying of the words, the same way it did when he forced a laugh for a bad joke. 'There are children in the Walsh house,' he said.

'I suppose there are.' The soldier waved his arm. 'Walk on, then.'

A whirr behind the cart made the soldier stand straighter and lift his rifle across his chest. The whistle they had heard sounded again. The soldier propped his gun along his arm and stepped forward. Malachy turned in a slow arc to see Patrick hove into view on his bicycle, the wheels sluicing through the ruts on the road.

'God almighty,' he said, under his breath, and glanced around at the others.

'Malachy,' Patrick called, 'Malachy! There are soldiers doing searches on the road near Tully. I came to warn you.'

The soldier raised his rifle and shouted, 'Stop!' Patrick, his eyes blinded by the rain, kept coming. 'You there,' the soldier shouted. 'I said stop. Stop!'

Patrick barrelled forward and the soldier aimed. Two shots cracked the air and the soldier fell. Patrick used his feet to slide the bicycle to a stop, he dismounted and stared at the man on the ground.

'You shot him,' he said, turning to Walsh, 'you shot him dead.'

'What the fuck else could I do?' Walsh said, his mouth agape, frozen to the road in the rain, in his woman's clothes.

The men moved quickly. They dragged the coffin off the cart, heaved it across a wall, shouldered it and made for the bog. Malachy and Walsh went to follow, hauling the soldier's body between them.

Malachy stopped. 'Go ahead of us, Patrick,' he said to his nephew. 'And don't look back.'

Patrick stared at Malachy but did what he was told; he hopped the wall and trailed the men carrying the coffin. Walsh watched the long back of him go before them into the grey. In the roadway, the wheels of Patrick's bike spun. A shot rang out and the empty cart rattled and grumbled under the rage of the sea-storm that did not want to let go of the land.

Penny and Leo and Married Bliss

Yeah, if you don't mind he wants breakfast in bed. Eggs. His Mammy always gave him a dippy egg when he was sick. Sick? Man flu is what he has. Have you ever heard of woman flu? You haven't cos there's no need for it. He only got sick, he says, cos he helped a wino find a bed for the night, and ended up jawing on Thomas Street with him for hours and it was pissing, of course. Sure when does it do anything else in this godforsaken country?

Still, I like that side of Leo, the kind part. He's decent. Never looks down his snot at the homeless or Travellers or Nigerians. But a wino? Go on out of that, I bet it was some hussy down in Blackhall Place he was 'helping'. Up against a wall. That man can't keep himself to himself.

Yeah, the other day Leo was on Facebook, on the tablet; I leaned over to see whose timeline he was gawking at and he tilted the thing away from me, the bugger. He had a laptop before but I destroyed it. I knew he was watching that auld porno and I was having none of it. So I got the computer and snapped the screen off the keyboard. I filled the kitchen basin with bleach and put the

97

screen in and glugged a bottle of stout in on top of it and a handful of Daz, just to see what'd happen. A wogeous smell is what happened firstly. I took the hammer to the keyboard – fwack, fwack, fwack! The whole thing was mangled. Was it satisfying I hear you ask? Did it help me out? It was one of the best days of me life.

He's a man you have to keep an eye on, my Leo. Loads of times I seen him and that Paulina making goo-goo eyes at one another, when she was here to wash *my* floors and iron *my* sheets. These ones come over from Poland or wherever with a mad hunger and they eat all before them, including our fellas. He said it was all in me head.

'Here,' I says to him, 'I mightn't'a' got me Leaving but I know a feckin slapper when I see one.'

Yeah, Paulina had to go. She was raging when I gave her her notice, yammered at me in Polish or whatever. '*Doopeck, sookah, hooey,*' she roared. It sounded like a load of me-ankles. Codology, as me ma would say. Doopeck schmoopeck.

Anyway, Leo comes across the bed after me that night and he's all talk.

'Who're ya thinking of?' he says, me knowing *he* has that Paulina in his head, with her little pixie face and dolly eyes. 'Who're ya thinking of?' he says again.

'Herman Van Rompuy,' says I.

He groans. 'Who else?' he calls, and he's bucking into me.

'What's-his-name,' I say, trying to think of the dirty Eyetalian. 'Him. Your man, What's-his-face.'

'Jaysus. Who? Who?' Leo's losing his rhythm.

'Oh, that fucker. The Eyetie.'

'Pope Francis?!'

'No, no, the other fella. Berlusconi, that's it. Silvio Berlusconi.'

'Aw, yeah,' he says, moaning and humping. 'Who're ya thinking of?' he says, as if it's the first time he's said it. Nothing will stop him 'til he's done, never mind me.

'Mahmoud Abbas,' I say, and that finishes him off. A big, fat groan and he rolls away, mucky with sweat, leaving me in the wet spot, like always.

I wish some fella would grab me sometime, in front of him, and kiss the face off me. That'd shake him. The new parish priest would do, Father Boylan. Such a waste of a good-looking man! All the aul wans are like dogs after him, gicked up to the nines for Mass and tripping over themselves to shove tea-bracks and naggins of Paddy into his hands. 'There you are, Father Boylan.' 'Did you enjoy the apple tart I made ya, Father?' 'Will I do you another of them bracks you like, Father Boylan?' Apple tart and brack me gee.

Oh, and he must be lost above in that fine house beside the church, rattling around its rooms with no woman to hold his head to her breast and say, 'There now, pet' when he's driven demented by the cardinal or the bishop or the aul wans. Ah, he's a fine thing, though. God forgive me but I'd bounce up and down on Father Hugh Boylan all night, given a chance. I'd pin him to the mattress with my two knees and show him what's what in the house of love. And I'd relish every second of it.

The rain is mad today, like a thousand nails hammering onto the sunroom. A blast of thunder frightens the shite out of me and I say a rapid Hail Mary. *Hail Mary, full of grace, the Lord is with thee; blessed art thou amongst women, and blessed is the fruit of thy womb, Jeeeesus.* Leo would laugh; he hates God and all about Him. I put up me May altar the other day and he snorted.

'Who are you trying to cod?' he says, nodding at the statue and the vases of bluebells I put either side of her. Me good Aynsley bud vases.

'It's for you,' I says. 'I'm hoping the Blessed Virgin will forgive you for doing the dirt on me morning, noon and night.'

That shut him up, but he came at me again later and, he must be on Viagra or something, cos he went on and on for ages. I was lying there thinking how us women suffer pain at every hand's turn: letting men plunge into us, pushing babies out of us. I was thinking too of Father Boylan which, despite all *his* faloothering about, Leo would kill me for. But what harm when Leo will never know? I was conjuring the Father, the way he lingers his eyes on me, holding my stare like a man about to declare his intentions. I look back at him the way any auld brasser would until he starts to wriggle. It's innocent enough but I betcha Boylan'd love a glim of me bosom, same as any fella. Man of God, how are ya?

For all his scoffing at me religious bits, though, Leo'll *plámas* me the odd time. Sure didn't he ask me to marry him by Saint Valentine's tomb beyond in Whitefriar Street, knowing I love it there? Though the next minute he ruined the romance of it all by telling me the soul is an invention, that there's no such thing! His mind is loopy like that, hopping from one thing to the next. To make it worse, as soon as he said that he put his paws on my chest, right there in the church, and the Black Madonna blushing scarlet on her perch above us. He has no manners.

Last week Leo says to me, 'Your fine Jesus was a carpenter.'

'At least he wasn't a doley waster,' says I, and then he was off on one about socialism, but I only back-answered him because he was dancing at the time with Josie – we were at Georgina's extension-warming – and the dance looked more like riding from where I stood, them stuck front to front like a pair of barnacles.

I was trying to distract him from Josie, so I called out, 'Didn't Georgina's builder do a grand job?' and that's when he said about Jesus and I don't know why he says half what he says, except that he takes pleasure in upsetting people. He's lucky I don't murder him half the time. And even though we didn't speak a WORD on the way home he's on top of me in the bed, quick as quick, and I says, 'If you put a bun in that oven, Leo Bloom, I'll strangle the life out of you.'

The last thing on this earth I need is another brat, crawling all over me. Thank God I only have the one, not like that drippy madser next door with her GAA team and twins on the way. Her huge, unholy bump is as much a part of her as the hair on her head. And she's always grinning like a loo-lah. I want to tell her they invented the pill cos I don't think she's copped that yet. The dope. She's not a total dope, though. Won't she be clearing a grand a month in Mickey Money soon enough? Nice if you can get it.

Still, she's better than the ding-dong on the other side. Your woman knocks in to me yesterday, half gone on smack.

'C'mere, Penny,' she says, 'will ya come in and get the vein on me fella? I'm after doing meself and I'm not able.'

I told her to eff off, I wasn't touching his poxy veins, and I says to Leo last night, 'Who lets madsers like that into a private estate? That fucking Council should be shot.'

Yeah, what I'd like is a house in the country, away from people altogether. That'd put a stop to Leo's gallop. He'd have no town to go to, no butties to lead him astray, no winos to help. And I'd be able to spend me day with nature: oaks, whitethorn, roses, bees. I love all that. I'd probably get fat though. It'd be car journeys everywhere instead of me fast clip through the streets of Dublin. I'd have to lay off me glasses of wine at night to stay slim. I could walk the lanes, I suppose, and enjoy the daffodils and snowdrops, but who'd see me in all me fine style? And I suppose Leo'd be bored off his head and, with nothing else to do, he'd be scrooching down on top of me all day, every day. Maybe there's worse things for a man and wife.

Here, I'll go and make his aul eggs. Poached with a drop of vinegar, the way he likes them. They'll come out all white and pink and yellow like Neapolitan ice-cream, as good-looking as hotel eggs. As good-looking as Father Boylan.

Ah, my Leo's not the worst. He's clean, I'll say that
for him – he's not a man to traipse muck over your clean
tiles. And he's good in the heart of him, in the soul that
he doesn't believe in. And at least he's mine and I know
him and he comes home to me at night. Yeah?

Room 313

You rap on the door and call out, 'Housekeeping.' You
don't wait long when there is silence. You want, sometimes, to swipe the key card and catch people doing
things that are the stuff of locked doors. The most you
have witnessed is a retreating bare behind, married to a
shocked 'Oh'.

You love business people; their hardly there-ness,
their generosity. Before you roll out your cart each
morning, you study your list. The list is your map for
the day – too many Leavers and it will be a tough one;
lots of Stayers means a soft run. If the Stayers are business people, even better: they lie on one side of the bed,
barely denting the pillow. They use a single towel and
don't mess with the toiletries. It's hoover humming idly
and TV on, a little sit down, then pluck away a few stray
hairs from the bed and bath, and job done.

You like families too; the other maids complain about
them – the walked-in sand, the chaos – but families leave
behind toys and you get to keep them for your girl. You
have taken home to your bedsit hardly loved dolls, sweet
picture books, and all shapes of buckets and spades.

The ones you hate are the lovers: these are the choco-
late-on-the-sheets brigade; strawberry hulls mashed into

the carpet; sticky champagne glasses and a sodden towel heap. They leave hairs clogging the plughole and floaters in the toilet; they are too distracted to flush. Lovers are slovenly, slapdash, and the bastards never tip.

All this week you are doing Room 313. Marta, the Head Housekeeper, says it's not normal for a hotel to have rooms with the number thirteen on the door and she refuses to even enter them. But Room 313 is your favourite, your lucky room. It is the room of the €100 tip that you kept secret because the other girls would talk too much about it if you told them. And then Marta would sweep the rooms before you begin each morning, vacuuming up your tips; she would lose her thirteen phobia pretty quick, you reckon. Ever since the €100 tip, you've loved this room; it seems to hum with energy.

Its current occupant is a business woman; you have christened her Coco. All her clothes are black and white; her underwear too. She wears black slips with white piping that feel soft as baby skin beneath your fingers. Even softer when you slip out of your uniform and try them on. Coco's perfume is citrus sweet and comes in a tiny metal flask that you have to wipe down after you try a spritz because your fingerprints smudge the silver.

You stand at the window of Room 313 and look down. It rains all the time here, a roof of grey covers the place and rarely lifts. Even the sea is dark – it churns and turns, a murky broth. You think of your daughter and wonder what her voice sounds like now. She is silent on Skype these days, staring at you as if you are a stranger. Your mother says she is a great talker but you have not heard a word from her mouth for months. You miss her in a way that did not seem possible when you left Yalta. You would give anything to hold her small body in your arms and place her in bed for the night; rub her back until she drifts. You would love to see her wake with candyfloss hair and one pudgy paw under her cheek.

Room 313 has a peacefulness that makes you linger. You turn from the window and begin a half-tidy; Coco doesn't cause much mess. You pull the bedcovers straight, fix the curtain pleats and empty the bin. You stay a while in her room, sitting in the chair by the window, enjoying the comfort of the space, the calming view of the sea-shore. 313 always smells nice, no matter who stays in it; the hotel's corridors are sour and they make your stomach flip-flop. You think how you would like to bring your daughter to the beach – here or at home – and let the water lap her toes. Together you could claw the damp sand with your fingers and make a mighty sand-castle.

You are sitting on Coco's toilet when you hear her come in and you have to suck the poo back inside and pretend that you are washing the sink, so she doesn't suspect. You open the bathroom door and she stands there, staring.

'Oh, it's only you,' she says, and laughs. She opens the window and lights a cigarette. 'I'm the solo smoker at the conference. I feel like a pariah, so I come up here to have a fag. Want one?'

You shake your head. 'I will come back later; I was nearly finished anyway.'

'No, no. I won't get in your way.'

You take your can of Mr Sheen and start to spray and dust the wardrobe doors, knowing that she is following you with her eyes. The cigarette smoke blends with the Mr Sheen and with her perfume, newly scenting your skin.

Coco goes to the safe and taps in her code; the safe lows like a calf as it swings open. She takes out a pearl necklace and holds it up.

'What do you think of that?' she says.

'Pretty.'

'Come here. Try it on.'

'Oh, no. I couldn't.'

'Please,' she says, and points to the mirror, so you stand in front of it.

She moves behind you and you feel heat radiating from her body. Her hands come around your front and she unbuttons the top of your uniform. She lays the cold pearls against your throat and snaps the clasp.

'Look at them, like a row of moons,' she whispers, close into your ear. 'They come from the Gulf of Mannar. Imagine the diver, naked, plunging to the ocean floor. Imagine him shucking open the oyster, looking for that lunar glow.' Her eyes are locked onto yours in the mirror. 'Imagine how many times he had to dive through the deeps to find each pearl on this string.' Her hand moves across your breastbone, fingering the beads one at a time. 'Where do *you* come from?' she says.

'Ukraine.'

'I knew you were too good-looking to be Irish.'

Coco lays her hands on your shoulders and you feel like a bird, safe under its mother's wings. She dips her head and her lips are on your neck; you can feel the soft wetness of her tongue; she licks at your skin then bites gently with her teeth. You close your eyes and feel everything swell between your legs.

In one swift jerk, she steps back, unclips the pearls and marches towards the safe. She throws the necklace inside, slams the door and punches in her code.

'You never know who'd be wandering around your room,' she says, grabbing her handbag from the chair and leaving.

Your skin shines where her mouth was. You run your forefinger across the wet patch then lick it. With the same finger you press the digits on the safe's keypad. Once again it gives an animal groan. You take the pearl necklace and pop it into the pocket of your uniform. With it you pocket the diver and his shucking tool, the oyster shells and sunshine and clear green sea of the Gulf of Mannar. You turn off the light and close the door on Room 313. The grains of sand that the pearls once were, safe now, in your hands.

Mayo Oh Mayo

Tonight there is a moon-rind, a nicotined fingernail, hanging low over the lake; above it, a Swarovski sparkler of a star. The three seem aligned – moon, lake and star – in some perfect ternion of universe, mood and happenstance, their very threeness a sign of good things. The car streams forward transforming Siobhán's view of all three and each different aspect embeds their power deeper into her.

What celestial abandon gave rise to this? Siobhán recites to herself. This is a favourite quote and she murmurs it often, hoping to find some situation where it will be one hundred per cent appropriate, one hundred per cent appreciated. She could say it out loud now, to see if her American man reacts in a pleasing way, but more than likely he won't. Siobhán turns to gaze at him; she likes that she can see him despite the dusk-light of the car as he drives this bog road.

He is embarrassingly American, this man: close-shaven, white-shirted, hair inert as a doll's. And he is as hard to read as any Irish man, but without the soft edges of ready laughter, the softer edges of drunkenness. His manner is aloof; he carries a permanent aura of loneliness. Does this, she wonders, mean he is a loner, or a maverick, or is he just plain standoffish? He is driving her home, both belly-full after a dinner in a castle in the next county, and he will come into her bed tonight, into her.

Siobhán turns back to the view. The lake wants to pull the moon into its depths, it croons like a siren, but the star keeps the moon in place, pinning it to the navy sky.

'What celestial abandon gave rise to this?' she says at last, keeping her voice low.

'How's that, Siobhán?'

'Oh, it's nothing really. A quote.'

'Shakespeare?' He turns to her and exposes his good American teeth in a smile, then returns his eyes to the road.

'Not every snappy sentence is Shakespeare. If you really want to know, it's a line from a story about a baby with cancer.'

'Wow, Siobhán. Happy.'

She shakes her head. 'Never mind.'

'OK.' He takes his hand from the steering wheel and places it on her leg; Siobhán locks her fingers through his – a wifely manoeuvre, she thinks.

Being in the passenger seat of her own car makes her jumpy, the dimensions of the space have shifted and it feels like she is sitting on an outcrop. The road seems extra narrow, the ditch too close. She looks out the window but the moon-slice is hidden now behind a scarf of cloud and the last lip of the lake is behind them.

The man's name is Conrad, like the hotel chain, as he said when they were introduced. She has tried to call him Con but he won't have a bar of it.

'Conrad. Please,' he has said, more than once, and she imagines him performing this little whine with everyone he meets.

She is glad of her own name and she likes the way he repeats it when he addresses her. *Siobhán, Siobhán, Siobhán.* Irish men don't say your name, or never with such care, such emphasis.

★

She had walked him around her hometown in Laois. They ambled the streets, he noting, she felt, every collapsing gutter, every whited-out shopfront, the plethora of drab drapers.

'It's so different,' he said and she agreed that it was. Different to Dublin, different entirely to the States.

She spotted her granny coming out of the butcher's and breathed a low 'Fuck.' There was no escape route and, anyway, Granny saw her and came barrelling along to see what she could find out. Siobhán stopped, kissed her grandmother, and stepped back.

'This is Conrad, Granny. This is my granny. Alice.'

'Pleased to meet you, ma'am,' he said, and shook Granny's hand.

'Conrad's from America. Chicago.'

'Yes.' Granny cocked one eye at Siobhán, then studied Conrad. 'I hope she's showing you more than the insides of pubs.'

'Oh, we've been to Trinity College. And beyond.'

'Enjoy yourself now,' Granny said to Conrad; she nodded at Siobhán and walked on.

'I'm in for it,' Siobhán said.

Granny rang the house that evening.

'I nearly burnt down the church,' she said, 'I lit that many candles for you.'

'Why was that, Granny?'

'You know well why.'

'Do I?'

A pause. 'Where did you get the Yank?'

'America.'

Granny sucked air through her lips, a long-familiar, derisive sound with many meanings. 'He has hair to sell. I'll give him that.'

Siobhán looked at Conrad, where he sat on the bed beside her, at his thick, dark hair. 'He has.'

'He's married, Siobhán.'

'What makes you think that, Granny?'

She tutted. 'Isn't it written all over him?'

'It could be worse, Granny; Conrad might be from Dublin. Or, worse again, I could be up the duff because of some random Dub.'

'If you became an unmarried mother we could get rid of it. This is here for everyone to see.' She grunted. 'Walking him down Main Street like a prize bull.'

'Ah, Granny.' Siobhán sniggered, but felt glum once she had hung up. Conrad rubbed her back for the duration of the phone call and after it.

'She'll get over it, Siobhán,' he said. 'It's just generational, she'll come round. Funny, I never imagined we might bump into your relatives. One of your students, maybe, but not family.' He leaned in and kissed her neck. 'I bet the boys are hot for teacher.'

'I'm the saddo science nerd back in Smalltown. There is nothing remotely hot about that.'

Conrad kissed her full on the mouth, made a rope of her hair with one hand and tugged it. 'Why don't we leave here, take a road trip? Head west.'

'OK,' Siobhán said. 'Why not?'

★

He is childlike in sleep, this man of America, all properness abandoned with limbs akimbo and tiny farts released like whispers. She watches the fretful throb of his pulse and wonders if he dreams. He doesn't talk much or, rather, he talks plenty but doesn't say a lot. Nothing about his wife or daughter, little about his lab work, zero about how he feels. Nothing much about anything. Is he, Siobhán wonders, the most restrained man on the planet? Would you call him taciturn, even? She wonders why she likes him at all. What's to like? His Gitanes-blue eyes, maybe. That crop of black hair. The very reticence that also drives her mad, because there is comfort in his silence, in the absence of detail and, therefore, knowledge.

Siobhán gets up to use the toilet; it surprises her that the hotel room has the same sour, feral smell of any morning bedroom. She pees, returns, and clicks open the window; she fancies she hears the rush of the Shannon over a weir, but maybe it is only the Athlone traffic advancing on the town to rouse it. The marina sits below the window and already there are sailors readying their boats for the day. It is June and the light has been good for hours. She looks up – the sky is a lid of planished zinc but no rain falls.

She slips back under the quilt and Conrad wakes, squinting one eye to study her. He smiles. 'Hey.'

She holds up her mobile to show him the weepy-cloud icon on the screen. 'My phone is raining.'

'What's new?'

'It's dry outside, though.'

Conrad is irritated by the poor Irish weather; fed up with its constancy and soak. Is he irritated with her too? She has concluded that he doesn't like Ireland much and, by extension, Irish people. He had an idea of the country – ancestral, genuine – that has not lived up. He was very Emerald Isle about it when they first met in Chicago. Siobhán had tried to lay out some realities before him: drug wars, high unemployment, dormitory towns, asylum seekers left to rot in camps, the poor getting poorer, rampant corruption etcetera. But he chose not to hear, or, not to believe her. Then, in Dublin, he was shocked by Starbucks on Westmoreland Street; he stood outside it for a whole minute to allow himself be fully offended.

'You guys have Burger King,' he said, on another of the Dublin days, and it was an accusation.

'We have credit cards too,' she said, and he snorted lavishly, this Midwest-via-Florida man, with his pristine manners and spotless self. He snorted often, so she didn't take offence, it seemed to be his idea of an acceptable answer to many things. She linked her arm through his. 'The far west of Ireland is wilder, more traditional,' she offered, as consolation.

Now Conrad pushes his hands over his face and through his hair. His physicality stuns Siobhán, the slender impeccability of it — he is lean, has lush hair in all the appropriate places and is freckled sporadically on smooth-as-milk skin. He is what Granny would call a well put together man. If she approved of him.

Conrad turns to her, his face close. 'Is obesity a problem here, Siobhán?'

'Here in this room?'

'No. What are you talking about?'

She runs a hand over the belly that she knows will never disappear because she will do nothing to help it. Conrad sees this movement and he tucks his hands into the small of her back to pull himself flush to her. He kisses her nose and presses her head to his chest, one hand tangled into her hair. He doesn't smell of anything — not sweat, not artificial scent. His non-odour makes her aware of her own smells: caramel feet after a day in runners; acidic underarms; the creamy scent between her thighs. How can he possibly smell of *nothing*? Maybe she has imagined this person, this stench-less demigod; her loneliness has conjured him out of the air.

'Do you want to have a little hot fun?' she says, parodying a Southern drawl.

'I sure do,' Conrad says, leaning back to look into her eyes. 'Great!'

He says 'great' a lot. 'I fancy some Tayto,' Siobhán might say.

'Great,' he'll reply.

'Let's go to the round tower in Glendalough; it's a phallic wonder.'

'Great.'

'This is the Book of Kells.'

'Great.'

Despite all the greats, she feels Conrad is not charmed enough by her country's assets, or she is not doing a sufficient job of unveiling them. Nothing is really as great to him as his repetition of the word might imply. She wants to try harder.

'You're not easy to impress,' she said, in the Long Room library in Trinity College, when he gave the Book of Kells an impassive gander. He stared at her and said nothing, but he moved his pelvis into hers and put his lips to her mouth, then a lizard flick of the tongue that she grabbed at, curling her own onto his until both were engrossed in the kiss, hooked there, his groin pushed against her in the middle of the library. They stayed there for moments, aware of the mob of tourists flanking them, determined to see the monkish luminescence that had lured them. But Conrad ignored the mill of people and stayed where he was to kiss her and she loved him for that.

★

'What about Sliggo?' Conrad says, studying the map on his phone at breakfast.

'It's "Sligo",' Siobhán says, trying to cut edible corners off a greasy hash brown.

'Sliggo, Sligo. Potato, potato.'

'Except no one says potato, the same way no one says Sliggo.'

Conrad shrugs. 'Anyway, let's go there.'

'I feel I should warn you, it never stops raining in Sligo. I mean *never*.'

'It never stops raining anywhere in Ireland, so what's the difference?'

Conrad drives again and Siobhán slumps in her seat watching cat-fluff clouds and the skein of jet contrails. The ditches are summery with squads of pink valerian and buttercups, cow parsley and ox-eye daisies.

'Did you know,' she says, 'that "daisy" was originally "day's eye"?'

'I did not know that, Siobhán. Hah.'

'I suppose the yellow centre was the sun.'

'Sure.' Conrad nods.

'The all-seeing sun.'

He taps the steering wheel and keeps his eyes forward, the road, apparently, more alluring than conversation.

★

Sligo does not excite Conrad much.

'It's very small for a city,' he says.

'Small is good,' Siobhán says. 'And anyway, it's a town.'

Even the combed flank of Ben Bulben, the mystic hulk of it, does not seem to move him. Siobhán can feel her ire nest and sprout like a pit in soil. But it is mixed up with her lust for him, which is a constant jangle, and forgiveness comes with that. She scrabbles for fresh wonders to lay out before him – kite surfers at Rosses Point, the Metal Man lighthouse, the bronze woman mourning those lost at sea. He likes it all well enough but his restraint about everything – except sex – is starting to rile her. She casts around for fresh diversions and a roadside *pietà* near Drumcliff becomes a signal to her for where they should go next.

'Let's head south of here,' she says.

'Great,' Conrad replies.

He turns the car and Siobhán sets the satnav. The place names on the way are bewitching and they recite them to each other.

'Curry.'

'Curryfule.'

'Cloughvoley.'

'Lismaganshion.'

'Meeltran.'

'Shanvaghera.'

'Addergoole.'

'Sallyhernaun.'

'Cloondace.'

'Knock.' Conrad giggles. 'Knock-knock, who's there?'

'Knock-kneed.'

He splutters, 'Knock-kneed who needs knocking-up in Knock.'

'Knockers,' Siobhán says, scrunching her hands in front of her breasts.

'Knock,' Conrad repeats. 'I really can't get over that.'

★

Knock Conrad likes. Knock, County Mayo, the time-warpy, priest-bejewelled village of Ireland's most notorious BVM hallucination.

'Now you're talking,' he says, and walks the place with a beatific smile, taking everything in. He dips into religious shops and pauses at each stand to examine the contents: scapulars, statues, holy medals and water fonts. 'Wonderful,' he says, fingering a twirl of glass rosary beads.

At the Apparition Chapel they watch a Mass-in-progress through the huge windows; the priests are Asian, the congregation enormous. They see other people – pilgrims – put their hands to a section of the chapel's exterior wall and pray. Conrad queues up to do the same; Siobhán stands back. He closes his eyes and presses his hand to the brick, like a man possessed and grateful for it.

'Are you even Catholic?' she asks when he returns to her.

'Yes. Well, no, not practising. My daughter goes to Catholic school.'

His daughter, ah. So he does think of her; she who lives so far away, she who sprung not just from his wife, but from him. Siobhán shakes her head to rid herself of the lit-up image of his family, a trio that holds in her mind, a perfect, luminous ternion.

They walk on through the grounds of the shrine, drawn with the crowds toward the grey-spired basilica.

'Look at it,' Siobhán says, 'the Titanic of churches.'

'They spent eight million on it,' he tells her, more than a soupçon of approval in his voice; she is clapper-clawed into silence. How does Conrad know this exactly?

'Eight million? Eight fucking million on a basilica and there are families who can't afford rent and are living in cars?'

He snorts. 'Wiki says the village hosts a Christian rave at Easter-time. Could that be true?'

Siobhán shakes her head. 'Now what do *you* think, Conrad?'

She links his arm and they wander into the church; they stop at the largest Virgin statue.

'She reminds me of you,' he says.

'What? Of *me*?'

'The same melancholy.' He points to the Virgin's face and stands contemplating her with reverence.

'I need to get you out of here,' Siobhán says and drags him by the arm back out to the street.

Conrad insists on exploring yet more tat shops. He buys a mug with 'Póg mo thóin' inscribed on it. She wonders if its bare-arsed leprechaun will be a talking point in his Chicago tea-break room; she imagines him regaling his colleagues with talk of Knock, relating its charms. She buys a tiny rainbow-robed Jesus for the dashboard of her car.

'Why?' he says.

'I like that he looks gay.'

'Again, why?'

She shrugs and pockets the Jesus. Conrad grabs at her fingers and they walk hand in hand through Knock.

'Showcasing our unhallowed union in the presence of the holy hordes,' Siobhán says.

He stops, takes her shoulders and kisses her full on the mouth, causing a welcome surge between her legs.

★

Their B&B is called Divine Mercy, which delights Conrad. He goes to explore the house while Siobhán lies on the bed, her body weighted down by a dinner of pork belly and turnip. Conrad returns to their room holding a statue in a red gown.

'Look, it's Madonna of the Pomegranate! The family has a huge collection of different Marys. They're everywhere.'

'Put that back,' Siobhán hisses, she sits up and shoos him out of the room. Her mobile rings and she whispers, 'What?' into it.

'Why are you whispering?' It's Deirdre, her sister.

'Because I'm in a fucking B&B in fucking Knock.'

'Jesus Christ. Why?'

'Never mind why. What do you want?'

'It's Granny, Siobhán, she had a fall. She's above in the hospital. Mammy said to ring and tell you.'

'Oh God. Is she bad?'

'She might be. Mammy sounded shook but she wouldn't really say. She wants you to come.'

When Deirdre hangs up Siobhán skitters along the B&B's corridor, looking for Conrad. He is in the lounge, talking to the landlady; she can hear him through the glass door.

'We really love Knock,' he says.

'Isn't that marvellous? But your wife, now, she's Irish, isn't she?'

'My wife?'

They both turn to look as Siobhán enters the room. Conrad is perched on the arm of a chair, cradling a mug.

'I have to go,' Siobhán says. The singularity of that 'I' pings across the lounge and back to her, resonant as a tuning fork.

Conrad stands. 'Go?'

'Excuse us,' Siobhán says to the landlady, beckoning to Conrad to follow her back to their room.

'What is it, Siobhán?'

'Granny's in the hospital. I have to go to her.'

'Not tonight, Siobhán, it's too far. And it's late. The hospital won't even let you in. Am I right?'

She sits onto the bed, worry and exhaustion deflating her. 'I suppose. I'll leave first thing.'

★

Sleep does not come; Siobhán stares through the window. The moon is a fatter slice now, a nursery rhyme crescent with a butter glow.

'Poor Granny, I give her an awful time.'

'How so?' Conrad pulls her into him and she can feel the hard length of his cock in the small of her back.

'Granny doesn't like modern life to encroach on her world; she's the black and white telly, daily Mass, headscarf-wearing kind. I say things to shock her all the time but I'm embarrassed by it, as much as she is.'

'What kind of things?'

'Oh, stupid things. A few weeks ago I said "I think I'll go and get preggers, sure I can have an abortion in London if I decide I don't want it". But I blushed saying it. I do it to rile her, shake her out of her world, but Granny never answers, so my words always hang. Insincerely, you know? Ah, I don't know why I do it really, it's not very fair.'

'You're just reverting. You're back in your home-place and you feel you shouldn't be. I guess you were a teenager when you left?'

'Yeah. And I'm stuck there now. I wish I hadn't bought that fucking house.'

Conrad rubs her arm. 'You mention kids from time to time. Is that on the cards for you?'

'I'm not looking for a womb-filler, if that's what you think.'

'Thank goodness for that,' he says, and laughs a little.

'God forbid I'd ask you for anything,' she mutters.

'Look, County Laois is a lovely place, Siobhán. You can make a good life there.'

She turned onto her back, forcing him away from her. 'Like your good life, is it? Mister Happily-Married-in-Middle-America?'

'Chicago is in the Midwest, actually. Middle America refers to—'

'Oh, fuck off!'

'Whoa!' He flops onto his back and closes his eyes.

'That's right, blank me out. Make yourself blind. You don't know me at all, Conrad, and you don't even want to. If I dropped dead in the morning you wouldn't be able to say one true thing about me.' She wanted to tell him he didn't know himself either but the words wouldn't form.

'You're all wound up, Siobhán.'

'Jesus Christ, Conrad. Am I to be blamed? Just leave me alone.'

★

Conrad's flight to Chicago is the day of the wake; he offers to change it but she refuses. It's better this way; Granny would spin to think he was there, as if he belonged to Siobhán, as if he were a part of things. The candle heat in Granny's bedroom makes Siobhán queasy, and the tension and tiredness after Conrad's visit courses through her. So many nights of little sleep, of booze, of food, of aimless conversation and good sex.

She kisses Granny, small and snug as a baby in her coffin, and returns to her own house. The bed is still tossed from her and Conrad's last morning in it; the wine bottle has left burgundy rings on the bedside locker. Something he said in the car on the way back from Knock flickers through her mind; a comment about the Irish being full tilt.

'Roguish living is fun but tiring,' he went on, with a yawn.

'Would you like the joy bred out of us?' Siobhán answered.

So he was tired, ready to go back to the real world. Had he ever said anything kind to her, anything good or interesting, or deep? She struggles to remember and concludes that there is no getting to the bottom of the man because there are no depths to flounder in; Midwestern surface is all there is. She falls into a deep sleep.

★

Siobhán rises early for the funeral. The postman has left a parcel outside the front door, not wanting to disturb her; she heard him drive up, then away. She sits at the kitchen table, still in her pyjamas, and unwinds brown paper and screeds of sticky-taped bubble-wrap. There is a box inside and in it a statue of the Virgin, her feet on the ball of the moon, on her head a starry crown. Siobhán reads the card: 'I can't give you much but have this melancholic beauty. C x'

Siobhán picks up the statue, holds it to her breast and opens the back door; she is pleased to find the moon a cottony wedge above the house. She holds up the statue and studies the solemn, pretty face. Melancholy indeed. Clutching the statue by the base with both hands, she swings it back and forth in front of her chest, further each time so that she can hear it whoosh as it passes her ear. Finally, she launches it skyward, calls out 'Hail Queen of Heaven!', and watches as it plummets to the ground. The statue smashes against the footpath in a trio of satisfying chunks. Moon. Body. Stars.

Jesus of Dublin

I'm the O'Connell Street Jesus; I have a granite plinth and a glass case so swanky it could have come from the National Museum. My old box had a pitched roof – draughty – and I nearly passed out inside the PVC yoke some nut-job from Irishtown threw together. But this new box is the business: bulletproof glass, no less. Solar panels and LEDs for light.

The glass gets a bit foggy on a warm day, as if I've been hawing on it, but that gives me a rest. I let my arms down and shake them out. I normally only do that by night – 4a.m.-ish, when the last madsers are on the Nitelink back to wherever.

They hawk at me sometimes. Well, at the windows of the case. They fall around outside, wagging a finger and telling me how poxy the church is. I had one here last night.

'I can't stand priests,' he roared. 'Do ya know what they do to little kids? Do ya?'

He had a single from Cinelli's in one hand and a can in the other. He went deep down into his throat and sucked up a massive gollier to spit at the glass. Snort and *fwuh*; it landed, it slid, and your man staggered off, feeling like he'd done something big.

The mother's down the Bull Island doing her Stella Maris thing, watching over the sailors; it's peaceful there, she tells me – gulls and boats and wind. But I like the bray of the city; the thrum and swagger of it. Give me sirens and buses and neon any day. I'm high on the hog here, all right; Parnell behind me, the Spire before me, and Daniel O'Connell himself down the other end, standing proud.

I'm taking a long rest tonight; the auld pins aren't the best. Once I step down off the starry stone I do a few stretches, then park myself in the corner, back to the glass. Ah, I've a great life, really; there's not a bother on me apart from the stiff shoulders and legs.

'Arthritis,' the mother says. 'I knew that'd happen the minute they cut down those trees. You're too exposed.'

'Would you stop?' I say, not wanting her going on. 'I'm grand.'

She puts on the face then. You know the face they make, all holier-than-thou and don't mind me. She doesn't mean to be getting at me, but; she just worries.

Anyway, it wouldn't do if I was caught slumped in the corner dossing, like some laxadaisy idler. No, up I get, red robes straight, golden heart a-glimmer and arms cruciform. I have work to do, a city of people to watch over, because I'm the Jesus of taxi man and traveller; of Garda and gambler; Jesus of the pissed and the pioneer. I'm Jesus of culchie and jackeen; brasser and nun. Jesus of Nigerian and Pole; of wino and weirdo. Jesus of soft rain, December snow and rare sun. I'm the Jesus of O'Connell Street. Jesus of Dublin.

Shut Your Mouth, Hélène

The walking makes yellow blisters erupt on Hélène's feet. Primrose-coloured sacs of liquid, rimmed with scarlet. She bursts them at the campfire by night, after easing out of the boots that seem to shrink around her feet the further she walks. She does not complain to Maman or Papa, she knows what they will say: *Ferme ta gueule, Hélène. Hush! You are ten. Think of Ti-Pit and Ti-Jean – they are small boys. Do you hear them grouse?* It has been said more than once to her already.

All day they walk, a group of twenty, between adults and children, with one wagon for belongings, as well as a few horses and mules. The Connecticut River – and, later, the Merrimac – sparkles and spates beside them, a lure for Hélène's ruined toes and heels. She keeps her head turned to the water and imagines sitting on the bank to paddle her feet. She wishes she could swim naked as a trout through the river, the way she does in the Chaudière, with the *chutes* crashing above her like a million liquid angels tossed from on high. How she loves to bathe and dive in that river-pool below the falls. She misses her home in Lac-Mégantic; she misses Grandmère and her friends and the schoolroom. Yes, she even misses

the chickens and sows who caused her so much bother
with their greedy peck-and-snuffle.

'Does New Hampshire have a school, Maman?'
Hélène catches up with her mother and walks beside
her. She will talk to Maman as a way to unbalance the
hunger pains that claw at her belly.

'It has schools, *petite*, but you will not see the inside
of one, as you well know.'

Hélène pouts her lip. 'What will I be doing, Maman?'

'Whatever is asked of you, daughter. You'll carry
water, darn clothing, knit, spin. Any chore that needs to
be done.'

'I want to go to school. I miss my books.'

'*Ferme ta gueule*, Hélène! I have enough on my mind
without listening to nonsense. You know you are not to
speak unless you have something useful to say.'

'*Désolée*, Maman. Sorry.'

'Walk with your brothers.'

Every night at the campfire, Paddy Boyle sings sad songs.
Hélène does not need to understand Gaelic to know
that the songs are mournful. The tunes soar and drop
in such melancholic waves, and his wife's tears flow so
freely, it is clear the verses are full of sorrow. By day Mr
Boyle is an angry man. He beats the mules and snaps at
Hélène because she walks too close ahead of him when
she is mesmerised by the river's torrents that sing to her
like sirens.

'Get out from under me feet,' he bawls, making
Hélène jump like a scalded rat. His huge boot comes

scraping down her calf because she has dawdled too long in his path again. He yells at Maman, 'Missus, can you not rein in that child? She's away with the fairies half the day.'

Other times Hélène catches him looking at her, his tongue poked from the corner of his mouth, a furtive smile prowling his lips.

Mrs Boyle – Kitty – is a toad of a woman, wide of hip and flat of face. Her hair is cut short and Hélène doesn't dare ask Maman why. Mrs Boyle rides the wagon, perched on the back with her legs a-dangle, because she is with child. It seems to Hélène she sits there in judgment over them all.

One afternoon Hélène comes upon Mrs Boyle kneeling by the bank of the Merrimac, praying aloud. The girl likes the guttural, raw sound of the words: '*Go dtaga do ríocht, go ndeintear do thoil ...*' It is a language that seems to be scraped up from the speaker's gut before being delivered to the tongue.

Mrs Boyle's bonnet is on the grass beside her and Hélène sees the shorn head and also whorls of scabby scalp where hair is missing. It disgusts the girl but she feels sympathy too, for what is a woman without bountiful hair? Kitty Boyle snatches up her hat and shoves it on her head when she realises she is no longer alone.

'Oh, it's you,' she says, looking at Hélène. She ties her bonnet strings and attempts to get up. Hélène goes to her and allows herself to be used as a prop. Mrs Boyle leans heavily on the girl to get her footing, her breath falling on her face; Hélène is surprised to find it sweet, like Saskatoon berries.

'*Mo bhuíochas,*' Kitty Boyle says. 'I thank you.'

'Muh vweekus,' Hélène mimics, and they smile at each other.

'*Merci beaucoup!*' Mrs Boyle says, giggling a little at her pronunciation and looking to Hélène for reassurance.

'*De rien,*' she answers.

They walk back to where the others sit, alone and in groups, drinking from water cans and biting into hard tack. Hélène's papa gives the signal – a short blasting whistle through the teeth – and everyone rises, both keen and reluctant to begin walking again. The sooner they move, the sooner they might come upon a farm to buy eggs and milk. The sooner they eat well, the quicker they will gain the mills of Nashua, New Hampshire and the promised work. Then there will be money, clumps of it.

'Nearly two weeks,' says Mr Boyle, 'marching like savages.'

'Keep your pecker in your pocket, Paddy,' Jacques Aubry says, pointing at Mrs Boyle's swollen front, 'and you'll have less need for marching. Fewer mouths to feed.'

At first, Mr Boyle looks like he will thump Jacques but instead he lets a great, rowdy whoop and laughs for longer than is needed. Hélène looks at Kitty Boyle, enthroned once more on the back of the wagon, but her face remains unruffled, as if she has not heard anything that has passed between her husband and Jacques Aubry.

The moon slithers up over the trees, a silver coin against

the navy sky; stars hang in milky drapes. Hélène could spend her whole life watching the variance of the skies and be content doing it. She means to stay awake until dawn, to follow the moon's chase of the sun, but she falls asleep. Morning fingers its way up, dragging its fleshy caul, and the night-spell is fractured. Maman heaves herself towards the campfire and pokes at the embers, sending up ash in clouds.

Hélène takes the pail to the river and dips it low for water, lying on her front so she can pull it up by the handle with both hands. A movement makes her look into the river where she is astonished to see Kitty Boyle rise out of the water before her like an apparition. Hélène drops the pail into the river and has to scramble after it; she grabs it before it sinks and stares at Mrs Boyle, who is dressed only in her underthings. The material clings to her body, clearly showing the dark parts of her breasts and the swell of her stomach where Hélène knows a babe wriggles. The woman stands in the water and lifts her arms as if she means to flop onto her back and sail away.

'Mrs Boyle!' Hélène calls. 'Kitty!'

Mrs Boyle focuses her gaze and lowers her arms; she starts to wade towards the bank. 'I'd be gone but for you came,' she calls.

Hélène slips into the Merrimac and hauls Kitty out, half pulling, half shoving her. The woman seems not to want to leave the water, though it is cold. Pushing her onto the riverbank, Hélène squats and wraps her own shawl around Kitty's shoulders.

Mrs Boyle bows her head, holds her stomach and says, 'I'm all right now, *a leana.*'

132

Hélène is not sure if she is speaking to her, or the baby that grows inside her belly.

'Where is your gown? Your shoes?'

Kitty Boyle points to a stand of bushes and Hélène fetches her clothes. She pulls them on over the woman's wet skin and undergarments, dressing her as if she is an enormous doll.

'Will you tell?'

Hélène looks at Kitty. 'I know to keep my mouth shut.'

Mrs Boyle shivers and nods her thanks.

Hélène uses Kitty's mallet to pin down the Boyles' tent. Kitty stands with her hands tucked into the arch of her back, letting Hélène take over this small job from her. The girl is happy to help, pleased to relieve her new friend of some of her tasks. Thwack goes the mallet, deep goes the pin.

Mrs Boyle teaches Hélène how to knit in the Irish way. The girl's cables and diamonds do not look as firm and flowing as they should, but the older woman praises Hélène's effort before making her rip it all back and start afresh. They sit on the back of the wagon together in the evenings, their needles clacking companionably. Kitty tells Hélène about her island home in the East Atlantic; Hélène tells her about Lac-Mégantic and the river and lake she loves so well.

Paddy stands by the campfire puffing on his pipe.

'Have I two wives now, hah?' he says. 'With ye both at it, I'll be wearing a new gansey in no time. No time at all.' Kitty and Hélène raise their eyes to him but do not speak; they continue with their work, the rough wool piled in their laps. Paddy points with his pipe at Hélène. 'You'll get nowhere in life without proper schooling.' He stares at the pair for a moment, spits into the campfire and walks away.

Maman calls Hélène to help her wash pots and plates. Hélène leaves down her knitting and goes to her. They carry the utensils to the river and dip them in, scraping at them with clumps of grass.

'Don't be making up to the Boyles. They're not our kind.'

'They're here with us.'

'He's an agitator. A troublemaker. Keep away from them.'

'But, Maman ...'

'Hélène!' Maman claps two tin plates together. '*Ferme ta gueule.*'

The sun is a bright roundel in the sky but the camp sleeps on. Paddy Boyle passed around a few bottles the night before. They held something clear and potent that made Papa gasp when he slugged, but it unfastened his tongue. All the adults drank from the bottles and they sang, laughed and talked late into the night. Hélène tried to stay awake but tiredness from walking all day and the high heat from the banked-up fire made her drowse away, the voices around her becoming liquid and slow.

Now she knows the sun's morning heat will have warmed the waters of the Merrimac a little. She slips down to the bank, undresses to her skin and slides in. The river is still cool, yes, but its chill is friendly somehow, welcoming. A few strokes and she is clear of the weedy tangle of the riverbank; the current is gentle for it hasn't rained for a while. Hélène swims a bit, lets the water bubble over her mouth, flips onto her back and floats. She closes her eyes and lets the sun beat down on her face and body. She swims and drifts, eyes closed. In her mind she is in the river-pool of the Chaudière, bobbing towards the spray of the falls; any moment she will feel the first spritz on her face. Opening her eyes, Hélène sees that Paddy Boyle is above her on the riverbank, watching. He flips his suspenders down over his arms and fumbles with the buttons of his trousers. His hand disappears inside his drawers and he starts to beat himself rhythmically. His head jerks backwards and his mouth goes slack but he keeps his eyes fixed on Hélène. She bobs down to tread water and looks up at him. Over the sloshing of the river she can hear him grunt.

'Come here,' he calls. Hélène shakes her head. 'Come on, now,' he croons, stretching one hand to her while the other continues to work steadily at himself.

Hélène swims downstream, looking for a sheltered spot where she can climb out and get to her clothes. Paddy Boyle follows her with his eyes and doesn't notice the approach of Kitty or the mallet that she swings into his stomach. Paddy groans, pitches forward and falls face-first into the dirt. Kitty drops to her knees beside him, raises the mallet and brings it down onto the back of his head. The noise it makes is like the splinter of axe through wood. Kitty shoves her husband along the ground until he dangles over the riverbank. Hélène crouches in the water and looks up at her friend; Kitty stares back. She pants a little but she is as composed as a woman going about the keeping of her house. Kitty glances around, gives a sharp nod and Hélène wades forward and pulls Mr Boyle's body into the water. His blood-soaked face looms close to hers and she flinches and pushes him away. She and Kitty watch the Merrimac take Paddy Boyle with it, like a piece of driftwood.

Kitty offers Hélène her hand and the girl climbs from the water, sliding on the muddy bank. Mrs Boyle takes Hélène's pantalettes from the pile of clothes and helps her step into them. She pulls her gown over her head and fixes the sleeves as best she can over the girl's wet skin; she takes Hélène's hands in hers and stares into her eyes. Kitty does not speak but Hélène can hear her.

She nods to say she has understood and whispers, '*Ferme ta gueule, Hélène. Ferme ta gueule.*'

Girlgrief

'How do people in the graveyard get breakfast?'

Her grandad and I look at each other. This is the season of questions.

'Is God made out of sand?' she asks.

Kelly is four years old and we first met her a month ago, in Rättvik, at our son's funeral. Her mother is still in Sweden and no longer cares to raise her daughter.

Kelly watches us leave a room as if we're leaving her life. But she sheds no tears and eats little. She says the sourdough I make tastes of socks and walls. We coax preferences from her.

'Lingonberries,' she says.

'Pickled gherkins.'

'Curry and rice.'

We order Indian food and Kelly is pleased.

'Samosa is a type of pudding icing,' she says, 'so yum.'

We nod, baffled, but we're glad that there is food that she lets past her lips.

She calls me Granny and will sit by me in the house and walk beside me in the park, but if I try to hold her hand, she curls away, a coiled fern. Her grandad, she ignores.

I put her to bed in our son's old bedroom, thinking I will have to de-blue it now, for his daughter. I will paint the room primrose to welcome her, unclutter it of hurls and sliotars, the Che Guevara and cannabis posters, the photo-shrine to my son's long-gone teenage friends.

Kelly looks around at the grubby remnants of her father's young life.

'We'll buy dolls,' I say, 'and a Noah's ark. We'll get some Lego and a wooden tricycle.'

Kelly sits on the edge of the bed, an unyielding statue, and I kneel on the carpet, a supplicant before her.

'When I get married, will *my* husband die?' she asks.

'No,' I tell her. 'No, he won't.'

'Actually, he will,' Kelly says. Her seawater eyes dare me to contradict. She glances around the bedroom again and her tone lifts. 'Why did my Daddy have to turn into a magical dead boy? He's gone loco!'

I laugh, thinking this is what she expects, but she lunges forward and thumps my arm with her miniature fist. 'You're so bold!' she screams. She pushes her rage through her nose in spurts and stamps her feet, a tiny, feral horse, railing against her handler.

'Kelly,' I say, 'it's fine to be angry, it's OK to cry. I know you miss your Daddy.' Reluctantly, I add, 'Your Mommy too.'

I sit on the bed beside her and she climbs into my lap and looks up into my face; she puts her hands in mine and with them, I know, all of her faith.

'Cockhorse me to Banbury Cross,' she says, and I do, over and over.

'Horsey, horsey don't you stop,' she commands.

We clippety-clop and tail-swish until my legs ache and my throat is ragged. But I go on and on until she is my son, a jiggling, giddy, four-year-old, who finally tires and lies slack and sated in my arms. I hold Kelly close to my breast and cry into her hair. Great sobs gust through me and I shiver. Her arms reach to clasp around my neck.

'Don't cry, Granny,' she says, 'don't cry.'

I sit Kelly back on my knees and look into her face; it thrills me to see her eyes bubble over and the wet soak her cheeks. I pull her to me and rock her and we let our tears wash us clean.

American Wake

The Missus has a mirror as big as a door in her bedroom. I am setting the fire, as I do every morning, when I glimpse this nark-faced strap sneering at me from across the room. Who's that miserable one-een? I wonder, thinking another maid has snuck in. I look again. Of course it is myself.

'Merciful hour,' I say aloud, and stand up straight. It is amazing the way the face collapses when there isn't a soul to bear witness.

I go to the mirror; its big, gold frame glints in the gaslight. I dawdle in front of it and stare at myself. The uniform the Missus makes us wear is lovely: white and grey with a little cap, stiff as meringue. But that's not what I see in her giant mirror. No, what I see is my Mammy looking back at me. As true as God the eyes that look into mine are hers and the sad stoop to the mouth is hers and, to be nothing but honest, I nearly die. I put my hand out and the ache of seeing her, but knowing it is not her, is brutal. My Mammy. My sweet, foostering Mam is three thousand miles away in Galway and I am in Manhattan, skivvying for a so-called lady.

I hear an *olagón*, a deep keen of a cry, and it seems to come from far away but when I look into that glass again my mouth is twisted and the tears are walloping down my chest. I clap my hands over my gob to shove it all back inside myself.

The steamer I took across the sea was called the *William Penn*. A grand name for a grand boat. But I nearly went mad on it. They served us a grey slumgullion three times a day and half the passengers were wretched enough from that, not to mind the heaving waters and whatever aches and worries they had brought with them.

But the worst was the morning a boy from Ballinasloe was found frozen to death on the deck. Four years old he was. A baby, by any measure. He was going to join his mother in Illinois but the mad old witch, who was to get him safely there, left him out of her sight. The whole night he lay on that deck with no one to hold him, or comfort him, or warm him. He died from the biting cold; his tiny body got soaked through and went tough as a board. Maybe the poor craythur just gave up? It is a long voyage for anyone but, for such a little person, well, it must have seemed like there would be no end to it. His poor mother in Chicago will wait forever for her boy.

I stare at myself once more in the mirror; I am paler than I was at home. The food here doesn't settle in my stomach and the ache of missing them all cuts into me. I am thinner now, a shade of the girl who tripped up and down Nun's Island with a different man on her arm each month.

But, in the heel of the reel, I am here now and what is to be done about it? I thought I would never get out of Galway, out of Connacht, out of Ireland. One by one my friends and schoolmates went before me: to New York, to Boston, to California. I went to their American wakes and longed for the day I would have my own. My wake came and went: I danced my favourite hornpipe, I listened to the old people's advice and their wailing, and I felt happy, for I was in a mighty hurry to leave. But, now, I wonder, what was all my haste about? Did I really need to leave all behind to empty chamber pots, scrub floors and bake cakes for a house full of strangers?

My face is a shadow. My Mammy's features blur and slip out of focus. I put my hand to the glass and rub at it to try to conjure her again. And I am flattened by the truth of things: no more than the poor little maneen from Ballinasloe, I will never look into my Mammy's eyes again.

Storks

We are meant to be in Switzerland. We are meant to be staying in the hotel in the Bernese Oberland where I worked one student summer long ago. We are meant to be lording it over the Rüeggs, the handsome, humourless couple who ran the hotel. *More croissants, Herr Rüegg! Fresh towels, Frau Rüegg!* But we are not there because when I said Switzerland, Fergus heard Spain, and he was the one in charge of our escape.

It takes us a twisted hour to get away from Madrid airport and onto the right road; useful signs – no more than in Ireland – are scarce. But here we are, eventually, on a motorway that is flanked by squat olive trees and abandoned factories. Fergus drives; I enjoy the slump in my seat, the not having to talk. It has worn me out, all the talking lately – with the consultant, with friends and family, with Fergus. The endless going-over. I crave a muted calm now, just the two of us, in an elsewhere that does not include any points of familiarity, or long, tear-marinated conversations. Maybe, in that sense, Spain is the better choice; I have never been here before and we will manage to be properly alone, free of exhausting talk.

We head south because there is a place that Fergus thinks I will like. I am content to be a passenger, inert and quiet; content to be led. The fields to either side of the road hold skull-capped hay cocks and there is snow on distant mountains. I see static bulls with tails a-twitch that stare at the road from their fields, as if plotting a breakout. I know how they feel.

'Travel is always a kind of resting from the self, isn't it?' Fergus says.

'I don't know about that; I seem to haul myself with me wherever I go.'

'Well, that's understandable,' he says, 'especially when you're grieving.' He reaches over and squeezes my knee.

'As are you,' I say.

Fergus doesn't answer.

The air, when we stop at a roadside diner, is grill-hot. I had been craving Alpine air – Swiss-thin, Oberland fresh – when I decided we needed a trip. I know I have to make do now with Spanish air, but I am not altogether sure I can find the good in being here, the things that will restore me to myself. I have been squashed under the weight of this mourning; it sits on me like a lead brace and makes a dull, slack creature of me. The heartache is worse than when my mother died, though I haven't said this to anybody, not even to Fergus.

In a corner of the diner we eat tortillas, under the cigarette fug of the other customers – a row of desultory old men, stuck to barstools. When we finish, we drift across the room and stand in front of a glass cabinet that has knives and woven bracelets for sale.

'Weapons for the boys, jewellery for the girls,' Fergus says.

'It's like Aldi in miniature.'

We buy petrol in the Repsol next door – along with sweets and cold drinks. The garage forecourt boasts shelf after shelf of pottery piggy banks and phalluses.

'It's hard to know who those are aimed at,' Fergus says and we both snigger.

We go on. The Río Tajo shines like quicksilver beside the road and we eat greasy chocolate and thin, red liquorice sticks as Fergus drives us up into the hills. Four hawks dip and circle above the car. How do they see the dart of rabbits or rats against the dun soil, I wonder? Is the constant flash of vehicles – red, blue, yellow – not a complication to the hunt?

Fergus sighs.

'What is it, love?' I ask.

'Nothing, Caitríona.' He squeezes the steering wheel with both hands. 'Everything.'

'It's with me all the time, too.'

'I know it is, sweetheart.'

I close my eyes against the road, the preying birds, the Moorish fortresses that dot the hills, and ease myself back to March, oily with nausea and glad of it. Several times a day over the loo, puking lines of yolky stuff, the smell of piss and bleach helping the next heave along and the next one. I would get up from the bathroom floor, triumphant and dizzy, and sit on our bed in a trembly sweat, happier – though more nervous – than I had ever been. This one would surely stick. It had to, didn't it? When the sickness stopped I mistook it for a settling, a nesting-in. Then came the rusty spotting, followed by a torrent of red, and it was over. After that, sorrow, a defeated kind, because it was wefted

with blame and what-ifs and not-agains and a turning
against myself.

I open my eyes to a signpost pointing to Santa Marta
de Magasca.

'Will we go?' I ask.

Martha was top of our list for a girl.

'Let's just keep on,' Fergus says.

I see a tiny black pig on the hard shoulder. Roadkill.
It looks as calm as a cat-napper but it is all alone and that
makes my heart hurt. Little pig, forlorn and abandoned,
so very small. I turn away and face the road. The helix
squiggles of joyriders decorate the tarmac and I conjure
their hurtling madness on dark midnights on this moun-
tain pass, the exhilaration of it, the careen and skid, the
joyful danger. Maybe I will rob a car when we go home
and tear up and down the M7. Something – anything –
to jolt me out of this torpor.

We pass a solitary building stuck to a hillside; it has
two huge white orbs on its roof.

'Weird,' I say, 'they're like ping-pongs for giants.'

'Or a pair of eyeballs scanning the sky,'

'God is watching us.'

'Or are we watching God?' Fergus says.

'If he exists, that is.'

'Well, yes. There's that.'

Faith has departed me since our latest loss. What kind
of god would put us through this over and over? What
kind of god would deny us the one thing we yearn for?
I cannot fathom why I am being punished and I cannot
understand why my body won't do what it was made
to do. Fergus tells me time and again that we have done

nothing wrong, that it is nothing to do with gods or fate or sins or our pasts, or any of that.

'It's just biology,' he says.

Just.

Logically I know that he is right, but somewhere inside me there is always that nag, that scolder, who whispers that these losses are a penalty for some wrong-doing. That this is revenge.

I drift into a head-bobbing sleep, aware still of the car's movement, and dream a rush of things.

I am out walking a baby but when I lean into the pram, it is empty.

I am at an antenatal clinic and as the midwife palpates my abdomen it turns floppy like dough, a place incapable of housing a child.

A statue of Mary holds a teeny infant but when I stretch out my hands to take it from her, she pops it into her mouth.

The car stops and I jerk awake to Fergus saying, 'We're here.'

I yawn. 'Where's here?'

'Cáceres.'

★

There is a market on Plaza Mayor and I walk from stall to stall, buying pine nuts and *pimentón*, enjoying the feel of the cobbles under my feet after hours on the road. The stallholders are patient with my bockety Spanish, which morphs into German even for a simple thank you, the foreign language compartment of my brain all

muddled together. I have lost Fergus again; he is a rumi-
native tourist, whereas I prefer to take things at a gallop.
When I have exhausted the market, I look around for
him. He is on the church steps, talking to another man.
Fergus is animated, all smiles and chatter, and when he
sees me, he waves.

'Caitríona,' he calls, beckoning me over. 'Caitríona,
you'll never guess who I've bumped into.' He gestures to
the grinning man by his side. 'It's Worms Gormley, my
old boarding school pal.' He lunges into the man's side
and hugs him and they both laugh.

I have heard a lot about the elusive Worms over the
years, his story is so known to me that it's like meeting a
familiar: he is from Limerick, a nomad, a fiddle player, a
gas man. I shake Worms's hand and his look is quizzical,
appraising; he grips my fingers longer, perhaps, than is
needed and holds my gaze.

'Lovely to meet you, Caitríona.'

'And you. Are you on holidays?' I ask, taking my
hand back.

'This is home. I live here in Cáceres,' he says, scratching his beard.

'Nice.' I nod, already short of things to say. 'Do I have
to call you Worms?'

He laughs and slopes one hand through his raggy
hair. 'No, it's William. Will.'

'Worms wants us to go to his house. Meet the family.'
Fergus is delighted with himself, as if he has just pre-
sented a sparkling gift to me, but I am a-prickle.

'We can do that, one of the days, I'm sure,' I say, sending no-way signals to my husband with my eyes.

'When, Worms?' Fergus asks. 'Tomorrow?'

'Let me talk to Marta. Set something up.'

'Marta,' Fergus says, glancing at me. 'Such a lovely name.'

★

We share a *porron* of red wine at a café called Kiosco Colon. Fergus tries to make me laugh about the name of the place, but I am in no mood. We eat *jamón ibérico*; I savour its fatty salt until I start to think of the roadkill piglet and push the plate away. I sit for a moment, staring at the uneaten ham and then tears come – they are never far away these days.

'It was meant to be us, just us,' I say. 'Me and you.'

'I'm sorry,' Fergus says.

'I haven't the headspace for other people. You know that.'

'Come on, love. Worms is sound, it'll be grand.'

'I'm sure he's fantastic. No doubt his wife is a goddess. But I can't, Fergus, not in the state of mind I'm in. I can barely speak to you, how would I make small talk to strangers?'

He sighs. 'We kind of have to go now, Caitríona. It's all set up.'

★

The Gormleys have four children under four. Dark-eyed, red-haired, round as *puttos*. We sit in their kitchen and eat their food: cous cous with fat sultanas, smoked salmon, *patatas bravas* in a paprika sauce, stuffed *piquillo* peppers, and blue cheese that is the colour of cement. The children eat what we eat, to my amazement, and they are the most beautiful, well-behaved little ones I have ever met. They are all silence and enormous eyes, and they take us in with each mouthful they eat.

'Your kids are incredible, Marta,' I say.

Fergus looks at me and half grins, half grimaces. He knows I suffer around children.

'This *jamón* is great,' he says, 'we had some in a café yesterday.' He scoops more slices onto his plate.

'The pigs are so fat and flavourful, we call them "olives with legs",' Marta says, and we all laugh.

'We saw a piglet on the roadside on the way here.' I stop myself saying that it was dead; I don't want to alarm the children. 'He looked so sweet.'

'So sweet,' the oldest Gormley boy mimics and everyone laughs again. The child rolls his eyes, grins, and slides down in his chair, both thrilled and embarrassed by our attention.

Worms pours more wine and his eyes on me across the table have me squirming; he is remarkably interested in studying me and when I try to stare him off, he raises his eyebrows and smiles. I struggle to find things to say; I am flat and tired. My conversation is not much needed, anyway. Worms and Fergus want to reminisce about school in Galway and wild sessions in Tí Neachtain and Salthill. I half-listen, enjoying their buoyancy as they vie to remember their night-haunts, old pals and the details of escapades. It is good to see Fergus alight.

Marta rises suddenly, comes towards me and plonks the baby she has been holding into my arms. She rushes to mop up a juice spill that waterfalls from the table and threatens Fergus's lap. She gives out to the three-year-old who has caused the mess and Fergus protests and kisses the boy on the head.

He leans forward to look into the child's eyes. 'Beans and gravy,' Fergus says, 'that's you.'

'Beans and gravy?' asks Marta, wringing the dish-cloth into the sink.

'It's what you call a redhead with brown eyes.'

'When you don't call them Worms,' Marta says.

Her husband throws back his head and laughs. Looking at his face, I get a vision of a younger version of him on his back, clean-shaven, chest bared, grinning, me straddled across him. The scene is so vivid that I gasp and almost lose my grip on the wriggling infant in my arms.

'Take her,' I say, standing up and thrusting the baby at Fergus who grabs her under the armpits and looks in alarm to Marta. She comes, lifts the child, and tosses her expertly onto her hip. 'Excuse me a minute,' I say.

I leave the kitchen, thinking to go to the loo and gather myself. Was it Switzerland? Germany? Where was it? I stumble down a corridor, pushing at doors until one opens onto a hallway. I go to the end and land on a small balcony. The evening air is tepid but I am sweating; I look out over Cáceres and my heart wallops in my chest. The vision is clearer now: it was Switzerland.

Worms was the boy, my one and only false-hearted move against Fergus. Worms was the nub of guilt that

I had nursed and worried for years until, eventually, I managed to crumble it to nothing at all. I can conjure Worms playing fiddle in a corner of the Stella-Leone where my colleagues and I would linger each night after work in the hotel. I remember my Merlot-fuelled approach to a fellow Paddy, incited by my friends. Later, Worms – or Will, as I knew him – tiptoed with me up the staff stairs to my bedroom, both tittering and shushing, in my desire to avoid the formidable Frau Rüegg who might be on the prowl. And there were other desires, of course.

Homesickness had smothered me from the start in Switzerland – it was my first solo adventure, away from Fergus, away from my family. But it was something I wanted to do, to prove to myself that I was self-sufficient, or brave, some notion like that. When I realised that the red-headed fiddle player at the Stella-Leone was Irish, I was determined to talk to him, if only to wallow in the comfort of a familiar accent.

So Worms Gormley was my misstep. Will Gormley. Once, I had liked the fact of that lapse, that one night with Will. I enjoyed the covert feeling that I had something that Fergus was not privy to, could not own, and never would. The memory was mine alone. But I hadn't needed it after a while, so I let the memory go, ground it down. Forgot about it.

Cáceres's buildings are spread out below me at angles to one another, a fairytale tumble of red-tiled roofs topped with turret chimneys. I hold the balcony rail and listen to the town: an occasional car engine, music pumped from a bar and, above it all, an odd *clack-a-lacka-lack* that is followed by a prehistoric whistle. The sound comes again; it's like the rapid tap of sticks but hollower. Bones, maybe. The beating of bones.

I hear a door open and close, then footsteps along the hallway; somebody comes out onto the balcony behind me. I stay as I am, face forward.

'What's that noise?' I say. 'Listen!'

Clack-a-lacka-lack. Clack-a-lacka-lack.

'It's the storks.'

I turn to see Will. 'Storks?' I ask.

'Yeah, they nest on buildings and on the tops of poles. Anywhere they can get purchase, I suppose. Big twiggy nests. You must have seen them as you walked around the town.'

'I don't remember seeing them.' I turn back and peer out over the rooftops. 'Storks of all things.'

'Mmm.'

'What are they called in Spanish?'

'*Cigüeñas.*'

'*Cigüeñas.* What a lovely word.' *Clack-a-lacka-lack.* 'There it is again.'

'They're calling to you, Caitríona.'

'And why would they be calling to me, especially?' I twist my body to look at him.

Will runs both hands through his hair, a gesture I recall from that night long ago; I blush.

'Fergus told me what you've been going through. I'm really sorry.'

'I don't want anyone's pity. It is what it is.'

'It's hard on you, though. Childhood sweethearts and all that.'

I turn back to the view, strain to see the storks in the dim light, their nests. I think of Will's fiddle case, stashed under the bed in my staff bedroom, how I joked there might be a gun in it for all I knew, that he might be some class of Provo. I recall the sourness of his long-travelled denim jacket and T-shirt, the warm heft of his bare chest, the assured touch of his hands.

'Do you remember me, Will?'

He comes close up behind me and slips his arms around my waist. 'I knew you the second I saw you on Plaza Mayor.'

I swivel towards him and put my arms around his neck. We kiss and his mouth is soft and sweet, his beard a gentle rasp against my skin. His hands travel up and down my back, firm caresses that feel as if they might be the kind that could erode my cares. The storks restart their abandoned conversation: *clack-a-lacka-lack. Clack-a-lacka-lack.*

'They're calling to you, Caitríona. I mean it. Listen: "All will be well," they're saying. "All will be well."'

I turn from him to look out over the town; the dusk makes a peach–pearl sheet of the sky. I feel a push in my guts; something lifts and ascends and floats up and away from me. An evaporation. As the sun slips, my heart surges and I know, somehow, that I will leave this place in better shape than I arrived. Up from one of the chimneys rises a stork, all legs and beak, ancient, cumbersome and dark against the sunset. The call goes up: *clack-a-lacka-lack. Clack-a-lacka-lack.* All will be well. All will be well.

Acknowledgments

'Joyride to Jupiter' was published in the anthology *Town and Country, New Irish Short Stories* (Faber & Faber).

'Consolata' was published online in *Granta*.

'Yellow' was published online at *Cease, Cows* and subsequently in the anthology *A Box of Stars Beneath the Bed* (NFFD 2016).

'The Donor' was first published in the anthology *Lost Between: Writings on Displacement* (New Island) and subsequently translated into Italian and published in the anthology *Tra una vita e l'altra* (Guanda). Thanks to Zsuzsi Gartner from whom I officially adopted the opening.

'The Boy from Petrópolis' was first published in *The Stinging Fly*; it was subsequently published in the USA in *Guernica*.

'Napoli Abú' was published in *Crannóg* and in the anthology *Influence and Confluence: East and West – A Global Anthology on the Short Story* (East China Normal

University Press). It was translated into Chinese and featured in the anthology *An Encounter in the Global Village* (East China Normal University Press).

'Tinnycross' was published online in *Numéro Cinq* (Canada).

'Fish' appeared in *The Newer York* and in *Of Dublin and Other Fictions* (Tower Press).

'Futuretense®' was published in *The Lonely Crowd*. It was nominated for a Pushcart Prize.

'Squidinky' was published first in the anthology *Silver Threads of Hope* (New Island) and subsequently published in *The Irish Times*.

'Men of Destiny' was published in the anthology *Lines of Vision: Irish Writers on Art* (Thames & Hudson).

'Penny and Leo and Married Bliss' was published in the Irish Writers' Centre's anthology *A Telmetale Bloomnibus*, a 2013 rewriting of James Joyce's *Ulysses* by 18 writers; it was also published in *Of Dublin and Other Fictions* (Tower Press).

'Room 313' was published in *Five Dials 25* (Hamish Hamilton) and was translated into Serbian and published in *The Bunker Hotel* issue of Serbian literary magazine, *North Bunker;* it was also published in *Of Dublin and Other Fictions* (Tower Press).

'Mayo Oh Mayo' was published online in *Granta*.

'Jesus of Dublin' appeared in *The Chattahoochee Review* (USA) and in *Of Dublin and Other Fictions* (Tower Press).

'Shut Your Mouth, Hélène' was published in the anthology *The Long Gaze Back* (New Island) and online in *Guernica*.

'Girlgrief' was published in *The Lonely Crowd*.

'American Wake' was made into an art book and exhibited at the Group 8 exhibition in Ballinasloe in 2013.

'Storks' was published in *The Irish Times*.

★

Special thanks to my parents, Hugh and Nuala O'Connor, for always sharing stories. Thanks to The Peers – Mary, Patrick, Sara, Geraldine, Margaret, Lucy, Aoife, Alan, Maureen, Tony, Barbara, Gerardine, Jaki, Shauna and Noelle – who helped me to coax many of these stories along. Also my family, who have to weather the troughs as much as the swells. Gratitude in abundance to my agent Gráinne Fox for being a wonder. And to Dan Bolger, Mariel Deegan, Hannah Shorten and all at New Island who are the loveliest of teams to work with. *Buíochas ó chroí* to you all.